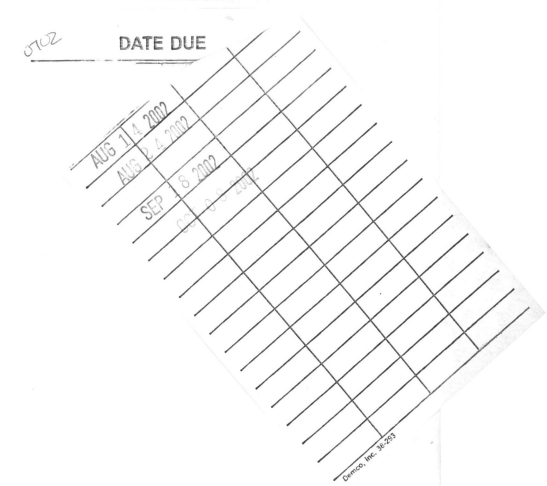

Lonesome Song

A Shep Harrington
SmallTown™ Mystery

Elliott Light

bancroft press

Baltimore, MD

Published by Bancroft Press ("Books that enlighten")
P.O. Box 65360, Baltimore, MD 21209
800-637-7377
410-764-1967 (fax)
bruceb@bancroftpress.com
www.bancroftpress.com
Also visit www.smalltownmysteries.com for more information

Cover design by Steven Parke, What? Design. www.what-design.com
Cover photo by Stephen John Phillips (Baltimore, MD)
Author photo and poor farm illustration by Sonya Light
Book design by Theresa Williams, theresa@visuallee.com

ISBN 1-890862-15-0 (cloth)
ISBN 1-890862-17-7 (paper)
Library of Congress Card Number: 2001086386 (cloth)

Printed in the United States of America

First Edition

*To the memory of Evelyn M. Light,
my mother and consummate story teller.*

Chapter 1

"**W**ho in God's holy acre is that?" wailed Sarah Mosby.

Her primeval scream reverberated through the small chapel, momentarily freezing me at its back. Robbie and Frieda bolted to Sarah's aid. I followed behind.

"Where's Reilly?" asked Frieda, Reilly's housekeeper, in apparent agreement with Sarah. "What's going on, Shep? Who is that man in Reilly's coffin?"

I glanced at Robbie Owens, Reilly's attorney, then stepped onto the riser where Sarah and Frieda were standing. I had visited quite a few funeral homes, and a lot of them recently, but I didn't recall anyone ever before questioning the identity of the deceased. The deceased on this occasion was supposed to be Reilly Heartwood, Sarah's younger brother. That Sarah had doubts about the corpse was no small matter. I peered into the coffin and gasped at the form stretched out in front of me.

Reilly had been sixty. His face had been creased by time and sun, and his head had sported wisps of soft gray hair. The man before me couldn't have been more than thirty, his hair thick and auburn. And there wasn't a wrinkle on his face. And yet, it *must have been* Reilly, or what remained of him.

A hand touched my shoulder. I turned to see a man in a dark suit.

"Good morning sir. I'm Jason Grubbs. You are?"

"Shep Harrington."

"Oh, yes," he said nodding, "you're the one that went to prison."

I had, in fact, spent three years in prison. That I hadn't committed the crime I'd been convicted of was a detail either lost on Jason or one he chose to ignore.

Jason turned toward Frieda and Sarah. Bowing slightly, he said, "I believe I know the ladies. My condolences to both of you." Jason Grubbs looked at Reilly lovingly, then said in a soft voice, "Hard to believe. That's almost how he looked when he was in his prime. Just like the album cover of his first gold record. Remarkable job. Don't you agree?"

Reilly Heartwood, known to his fans as C.C. Hollinger, had been a world-famous country singer. Why he adopted a stage name was subject to a lot of speculation, but no one ever offered any conclusive or convincing answers.

"I can't find the words," I said, staring into the coffin. For a moment, I considered throttling Jason for the irreverence visited upon Reilly. On another level, I was actually amused. Reilly had had a wicked sense of humor, and I could almost hear his thunderous laugh. I looked at Reilly again and realized how much I missed him.

Jason again beamed at the corpse in the coffin. "My wife's an artist. I wished we'd had the opportunity to do Mary."

Mary was my late mother. I nodded politely. I now understood why she'd asked to be cremated.

"I don't believe this," hissed Sarah.

Jason continued. "The embalming solution we use is our

invention. It adds color and makes the skin look life-like, don't you think?" Jason didn't wait for an answer, but reached over and pushed a button. At first, there was only a crackling sound, then the room was filled with the slightly nasal but melodic voice of Reilly Heartwood, known to the music world as C.C. Hollinger:

I sit here
and try and write a lonesome song.
You know it won't take me long
to tell you my mind, to tell you my mind.

I sit here
and try and find where I went wrong.
Where all my time has gone.
Why I'm alone again.
And how she loved me then.

Sarah, stepping forward, slammed her fist down on the button, and the music immediately stopped. "First I'm told my brother shot himself. Now you make him look like some kind of freak." Tears streamed from her eyes. "I want him to look like he did the day he died. I want him back."

"We all want him back," said Jason, restarting the music. Reilly's voice again filled the small chapel. Frieda helped Sarah to a chair and tried to console her.

I sit here
and think of all the words I might have said.

Like some sad book you might have read.
Memories of my past
Have me in their grasp.

I sit here
and try and write a lonesome song.
You know it won't take me long
to tell you my mind, to tell you my mind.

This time, I shut off the recording. "Can you fix him?" I asked Jason.

"I can't fix him," he replied angrily, "and I can't bring him back to life. Hell, I can't even arrange his funeral."

"What does that mean?" I asked uncertainly.

"It means the Reverend Billy can't give me a date for burial. It means someone will be paying me storage charges."

"And what is the problem with his funeral?" I demanded.

Jason raised his chin in a pout. "Ask Billy," he said. "I have no idea."

"You don't seem to care," I said.

"Reilly was a crook," answered Jason. "He didn't go to prison like you, but he should have."

My fingers rolled into a fist as a rush of adrenaline coursed through me. I wasn't offended by the reference to my stay in prison, but I wasn't going to let a slug like Jason badmouth Reilly. As I zeroed in on Jason's jaw, I felt Robbie's hands pulling on my elbow.

"You've got your nerve," said Robbie. I wasn't sure if she was defending me or Reilly, but I appreciated her effort nonetheless.

I made a quick feint with my shoulder. Jason jumped backwards and almost fell over Reilly's coffin, then slid behind Robbie for protection. "Like a lot of others in this town, I lost a lot of money because of Reilly," he said bitterly. "At least it was a lot to me. I was going to use that money to be someone. Here I am, stuck playing beautician to dead people. He cheated me out of more than money. His being dead is no great loss to me."

I looked at Reilly. "He did shoot himself. The medical examiner report was clear on that, right?"

My question was met with a silence that sent a shiver of doubt down my spine.

The question had been spinning in my thoughts the moment Doc Adams had phoned to tell me Reilly was dead of a self-inflicted gunshot wound. I didn't believe it then. I tried to argue the conclusion with Doc, but he dismissed my disbelief as "survivor's denial." I wasn't mollified.

Reilly had called me a few days after Thanksgiving. He spoke of "an epiphany" but didn't offer me any details. Over the next few weeks, he talked a lot about what he was going to do when his broken foot healed. At first, I was only politely interested. But when he talked about going scuba diving, a favorite pastime of mine, and about renting a boat somewhere in the Caribbean, something in me came alive and I started to pay strict attention. The last time we had spoken—again over the phone—was a few days before he died. He insisted I come to Lyle for the Christmas holidays "to share his exciting plans," which were too "complicated" to talk about on the phone. His enthusiasm was infectious, so much so that I got a haircut, shaved my beard, and packed for a week. First Doc, and now Jason Grubbs, were asking me to believe that a man with enough energy to pull me out of my funk would shoot himself a few days later. I just didn't buy it. "You're certain he killed himself?" I asked again.

Jason rolled his eyes at me. "I don't ask questions, Mr. Harrington. I just prepare the bodies. Apparently, some people appreciate my work more than others."

"What are you saying?" I asked.

"I'm saying that I have no idea how he died. There was no medical examiner's report. Doc Adams examined the body and the sheriff's office released it to me. He had a hole in his chest and an exit wound in his lower back. No way of telling if he shot himself or someone did it for him."

At the minimum-security facility where I served my time, I had learned to sense when things didn't add up. All the inmates there—me included—were supposed to be white-collar criminals, tax cheats, and other non-violent lowlifes. I soon learned that a good number of my fellow prisoners were actually drug dealers, pimps, and gang members who had entered into plea-bargains so they could serve their time at what's called a "Club-Fed" facility. In time, I could pick these bad guys out of a crowd or tell if they had a weapon simply by the way they walked or moved their eyes. After six months of incarceration, my senses were well honed. Maybe the hairs on the back of my neck would stand up, or I'd hear a low hum in my head. At first, I thought I was just paranoid, like many of the other inmates, but later I understood. If I felt something, I knew I had received data I needed to process. Here at Jason Grubb's chapel, I was getting signals, but couldn't fathom what they were telling me.

I recalled the face of one of the prosecutors at my trial. A witness had just lied to the jury about a conversation with me. My attorney's head dropped to his legal pad and the jury was nodding. The prosecutor looked over at me and gave me a victory smile. My fate had been sealed, and my education in how power is used was complete.

Now, I had an uneasy feeling that truth was losing out again. Doc seemed reluctant to detail how Reilly had died, or even entertain the notion that someone might have killed him. Without an autopsy, the official cause of Reilly's death was based solely on Doc's opinion. I knew Doc. I liked Doc. I even respected Doc. But there were times when his mental faculties failed him. If Doc was mistaken, then Reilly may have been murdered.

Reilly deserved to have somebody explore that possibility. Reilly had been kind to me all my life. As I glanced at his coffin, I realized that the "somebody" was probably me.

Jason looked at me pleadingly. "We both know that C.C. Hollinger's fans are going to demand stories and books about his life," he said. "I took pictures of him when he came in, and after we made him up. I've got the copyright on the photos; the estate has the right to his likeness. You get me a license to use the photographs and I'll split the proceeds with you. If you agree, my services are gratis."

I offered Jason my hand and he took it gratefully. I squeezed it until I saw the pain in his eye. "Don't push your luck," I said, then escorted the ladies to the car. On the way to the house, I told Sarah about Jason's accusation that Reilly had caused Jason and others to lose a substantial amount of money. I had heard various versions of this story and hoped Sarah would set the record straight. Sarah responded not with facts but by challenging Jason's heritage specifically and the rest of the town in general. Apparently, she was in no mood to be concerned with trees when she was busy burning down the forest.

I pulled into the driveway in front of Reilly's house. The morning fog had lifted, the sun was shining brightly in a Caribbean-blue sky, and a southerly breeze had raised the temperature to short-sleeve levels. Christmas was three days away, yet insects buzzed overhead and the few birds that hadn't headed south chatted noisily.

Robbie and I sat on the hood of my car and watched Sarah and Frieda go inside for a good cry. Robbie was my age—thirty-two—and like me, law school-trained and divorced. As I was growing up, my mother and I had visited Reilly often, making the trip from our house in McLean, Virginia outside Washington in Mom's old station wagon. Robbie was the only kid in town who ever came to play with me. She had aged well. She was a bit thick from shoulder to hip but pretty in an uncomplicated way. It wasn't hard to imagine her climbing trees or throwing a baseball in jeans and a T-shirt.

I felt Robbie take my hand in hers. This was the most contact I'd had in nearly five years with a woman whose name I knew. So, despite the solemnity of the occasion, I found myself thinking irreverent thoughts. Suddenly, I was seventeen years old again, back in Jake Lent's barn where Robbie and I solved life's most pressing mysteries. I squeezed her hand and considered renewing our old friendship. Then I felt Robbie's lips touch my ear and my heart raced. "I need to talk to you about Reilly's will," she whispered.

And I need to talk to you about the needs of a man who spent three lonely years in the slammer, I thought. "Sure," I said in my best mourner's voice. I promised that I'd drop by her office in the afternoon, then watched her leave.

Alone, I stayed outside and did battle with my guilty conscience. After Doc announced that Reilly was dead, I had seriously considered staying home. I was tired of people dying. I had been to Lyle to attend four funerals in less than twelve months. Last summer it had been my mother. The previous spring, three close relatives. The viewing, the wakes, and the services were emotional affairs. I hadn't been certain I could endure another.

I looked at the huge brick house and tried to imagine what it was going to be like never seeing Reilly again. The thought made me tremble, and I sighed it away. I wasn't ready to deal with that reality just yet, not without a few beers for company.

Turning my thoughts to what I had heard and seen at the funeral home, I revisited the questions I had about how Reilly died. Here was something I could deal with, and the place to start was the sheriff's office.

Chapter 2

Lyle, Virginia, population 3,650, is the county seat of Morgan County, a small splinter of land along Interstate 66. To the northeast, about forty miles away, is Washington, D.C. Front Royal, another county seat, is fifteen miles southwest. Reilly used to tell me that the problem with Lyle was that lots of famous people passed through, but none ever stayed so much as a single night. And no one of historical significance was from Lyle either. Lyle, as Reilly put it, "is surrounded by Virginia history but made no contribution to it." This, he said, explained the inferiority complex of the town folks and why they needed someone like him to carry the blame for all their shortcomings.

Lyle, at its core, is only a mile or so square. Three numbered streets run parallel to Main Street to the north and three to the south. Five named streets run perpendicular to Main. The town center is at Jefferson and Main. Beyond this orderly hub, Lyle is a labyrinth of streets that snake their way in one direction or another.

I walked slowly past townhouses of painted brick—whites mixed in with reds and creams—all adorned with colored shutters and solid wood doors. Along the street were the cars of the new settlers—Porsche, BMW, Mercedes. Like other small towns along the interstate, Lyle had been discovered by young professionals with lots of disposable income and not enough places to dispose of it. Whether it was the status of owning an old house or living in the country, or the quest for a small-town lifestyle, a wave of them hit Lyle about five years ago. Prices of a block of old row houses soared, only to fall when the price of gas and the reality of a forty-mile commute killed the craze. To Lyle's credit, many of the original renovators are still here, captivated, I suspect, by Lyle's panoramic views of the Blue Ridge, bucolic tree-lined streets, and old south feel.

As I crossed Main Street to the south side of town, I found cinderblock and wood houses that hadn't attracted the monied kids from the city. A few had been fixed up, but most showed signs of age and the limitations of their aging owners. Each had a small porch and matching yard. The vehicles of choice here were old Chevy and Ford pick-up trucks. Driveways of cracked concrete were littered with camper bodies and broken bicycles.

The house I knew best appeared before I was ready. For an instant, I saw my mother standing on the front stoop beside her mother. I remembered Gramma as a small, weathered woman who seemed to have lost half her height to a curving spine. She walked with a shuffle and her hands were bent with arthritis and the strain of days of grueling manual labor. Neither of the women talked about those times. By the time I was old enough to remember Gramma, she was too bitter to show me any attention. She died when I was eleven.

Caring for Gramma was my mother's most sacred mission and the mission I dreaded most. Gramma, who had cleaned houses for a living in Lyle and around the area, couldn't make herself clean the place where she herself lived. My mother did what she could to make conditions bearable, but the task was daunting. I hated visiting Gramma's house. Things thumped and scurried in the ceiling, and opening the windows never seemed to remove the stench of filth Gramma lived in.

While I was incarcerated, the fact that Mother had cancer was hidden from me. Only after my release was I informed of how little time she had left. Reilly came to her home in McLean and cared for her during her bad times. The job was turned over to me, reluctantly, and Reilly was either dropping in or calling every day. I often wondered why Reilly and my mother never fell in love. She was a widow and he was single. For all the time they spent together, I never once saw them kiss or even touch affectionately, but I sensed a bond between them. I was going to ask Reilly about their relationship, but now it was too late.

To be fair, my mother and I were not exactly close. I don't mean she didn't love me, but she had a myopic view of who I should be. She wanted me to grow up appreciating the plight of the poor and sick and elderly. As a consequence, even before my father left, I spent a good part of my childhood in Lyle away from my friends, especially during the summer. I was around old, sick, and poor folks more than I was around kids my own age.

One of her favorite causes was the poor farm outside of town. My assignment was to be nice to the residents, help them with their work, and treat them with dignity. I usually enjoyed my visits to the farm. A couple of residents adopted me, and taught me to ride horses and drive some of the farm machinery. I remember questioning why these lost souls, who had lived on the farm for most of their lives, didn't get jobs. When I asked,

Mom slapped me in the face. It was more than humiliating; it was a telling moment. If I were going to have a life of my own— with my own values and perspective—I was going to have to fight for it. Prison taught me the same lesson, albeit in a different way.

Now I headed back to Main Street and located the sheriff's office just across from the courthouse. I started toward the door, but walked to the end of the block instead. I'm not fond of police stations, courthouses, jails or any of the other components of the so-called justice system. To me, these institutions are more symbols of power than justice, truth, or fairness. I went to jail because the U.S. Justice Department determined that the company I worked for had committed fraud in its dealings with the Defense Department. The Defense Department decided that it couldn't afford to blacklist one of its contractors. A deal was struck, meaning that long before the case went to trial, keeping missile circuit boards in production was deemed more important than my life. People with families and kids decided that I should be locked up for twelve years.

These people lied about me, yet somehow slept at night. Investigators were sent out to prove that I had personally decided to defraud the government. And they found what they wanted to find, or made it up. Amazing!

Three years into my sentence, in an unusual turn of events, one of the witnesses recanted. Other witnesses followed suit, and the truth surfaced. I was freed only a few months before I would have been eligible for parole. I brought suit against my employer and against the government. I even thought about, but decided against, bringing in the Pope and the United Nations as co-defendants. I won a healthy settlement, but will probably have to sue again to get paid.

Our culture is funny about money. We seem to think that enough of it can make any injustice right. How much is enough for three years in an eight-by-eight cinderblock cube? In those three years, my wife divorced me, I was disbarred, and I lost my faith in humanity. Cha-ching.

၃၇

I indulged myself a moment of righteous indignation, then approached the sheriff's office, forcing myself back to thinking again about Reilly. As Jason had talked, an image of Reilly had popped into my head. Something was out of place, but I couldn't summon the image back. I was hoping the sheriff would be able to fill in the spaces, but I was predisposed not to believe him. The sheriff's office was a small square, divided at the entrance by a counter that ran the width of the room. A gate allowed access to two desks. At the back of the office was a door that led to four cells. Sheriff Belamy was sitting behind a computer terminal typing with his two index fingers. Deputy Sheriff Lou Tittle was crouched over the counter reading a newspaper and probing one of his nostrils with his little finger.

Belamy was a chunky man in his mid-sixties. A halo of salt and pepper hair surrounded his otherwise bald head. His jaw seemed undersized for the rest of his face, and his long thin nose and dark impatient eyes gave him an evil cast, as if fate had intended him to stalk a cemetery or haunt a house.

Fittingly, the last time I saw Belamy was in July at my

mother's funeral. He had distanced himself from the graveside service, but not so far away that I couldn't tell who he was. Only at the end of the ceremony did he approach me. All he could manage was a barely audible, "I'm sorry." He tried to say more, but shook his head and walked away.

The truth was, Belamy was an exceptionally fair man. He treated everyone equally, which meant no favors, no matter what. I have heard stories that in the late sixties, black prisoners from other counties asked to be jailed in Lyle because they knew Belamy wasn't going to mess with them.

Yet, for all that, Belamy remained something of an unknown quantity, a bit mysterious, a tad too self-sufficient for anyone to claim him as a friend. I liked him.

I approached the deputy, a moon-faced man in his late twenties. "Can I help you?" asked the deputy, reluctantly glancing up from his tabloid newspaper, but not totally removing his finger from his nose.

I wanted to say "no" but resisted the impulse. I looked at the sheriff, who was hunting for a letter on the keyboard, then said: "Well, I've got a few questions regarding Reilly Heartwood."

That got the deputy's attention. He straightened up and said, "He died," in a voice that reminded me of Dirty Harry.

"That's my point. I want to know how he died."

The sheriff looked at me but didn't speak.

"Why question good news?" said the deputy coldly.

Sheriff Belamy came forward and offered me his hand. "Hello, Shep. What makes you so interested in Reilly Heartwood?"

"Well, Sheriff, Sarah's pretty upset about Reilly's death. As you can imagine, suicide is a hard thing to accept. I thought I could settle her down by explaining the details of how he died. If I could see the police report ..."

"Well you can't," barked the deputy.

"Shut up, Lou," said Belamy. "There was no sign of foul play so there's not much of a report."

"Is dying with a bullet in your heart common in Lyle these days?" I asked cheekily.

The deputy leaned forward. "You want to know what happened to Reilly? He pushed his luck. He was living in this town like some God-damned celebrity, him and all his cats. He thought everyone would just forgive him 'cause he was famous and had lots of money. I think he cheated some people in Nashville just like he did here, only the Nashville types were big time. One of them put the squeeze on him and Reilly got worried. Being chicken shit all his life, he took the coward's way out and killed himself. Case closed."

Lou was within a few years of my age. He couldn't have known much about Reilly except what he'd heard or read in the tabloids. And yet he spoke with authority about Reilly's life.

"Could you give me a hint?" I asked. "What makes you think Reilly was in trouble with the hillbilly mafia?"

"I don't have to tell you nothin'," he said.

"Did you go through Reilly's papers or check to see if anyone may have had a reason to kill him?"

"You city boys get on my nerves," said Lou. He tossed his paper into the trash can, slammed the gate against the wall, and left.

"The Deputy seems a little edgy," I said. "Did you take away his one bullet?"

"He's like a lot of people around here," replied Belamy. "He sees people with money and knows he'll never have any. Makes him a tad resentful."

"Do you think Reilly was in trouble?"

"You mean that Nashville business Lou was talking about? No, I don't. But I believe Reilly shot himself. Maybe that's not what you want to hear, but it's the truth."

"Sheriff, does it surprise you that Reilly killed himself?"

"I've been doing this job too long to be surprised," he said. He went to his desk, then to the copy machine. "Here's the report and a death certificate if it makes you feel any better."

I thanked him and turned to leave, then saw Lou Tittle talking to a woman outside the office door. She was tall and a bit thin for my taste, like a lot of the models on magazine covers. "Tittle has a girl friend?" I asked.

"If he does, that isn't her. That lady's name is Amy Stewart. She's married to a lawyer who works in D.C. but bought a home out here. The lady tried to divorce him, but backed off. They don't seem to care what they say to each other or where they say it. Lou and I have been called a couple of times to break up screaming matches between them in public places. I saw the woman and her husband holding hands a few weeks ago. Go figure."

"Sounds like a marriage made in Heaven," I said.

"Can't say I understand why anyone'd take a city girl and leave her out here with no friends and nothin' to do. I've tried to talk with her, but she's a bit strange. Like she listens to you, but doesn't answer. Rumor has it she's a pill popper. Gives me the creeps, frankly, but Tittle can't seem to stay away from her. He thinks he might get her on the rebound." The sheriff laughed.

A moment later, Amy Stewart looked up. I was certain she looked right at me, and not by accident, before turning and walking down the street. Tittle, I surmised, was shooting off his mouth about me and my interest in Reilly's death.

I turned back to the sheriff. "Did you go to Reilly's house the night he died?"

Belamy hesitated. "Lou took Doc's call. He ..."

"You're saying Doc Adams discovered Reilly's body?"

"It's in the report. Doc went to visit Reilly and found him shot. He tried his best to revive him, but there was nothing he could do. By the time I arrived, Doc had Reilly all laid out, waiting to send him to the funeral home. Wasn't much for me to see. Based on Doc's statement, I had no reason to suspect foul play."

I glanced at the report and again asked, "Would it surprise you if someone shot him?"

This time the sheriff pursed his lips and answered differently. "I'd have thought someone would've shot him a long time ago. It looks like Reilly saved them the trouble."

As I peered up and down Main Street, I knew Robbie was waiting to talk to me, but a conversation about Reilly's will was not exactly what I had in mind.

Chapter 3

Sarah, Reilly's big sister, lived in Lyle's northwest quadrant on Monroe Street. Monroe was lined with ancient maples and oaks that, when in leaf, created a canopy that only a dapple of light could pierce. The small brick and stone houses along the street were fronted with deep lawns and azalea beds. In the spring, Monroe Street was alive with color, Sarah's house being one of the most impressive.

Not so today. Despite the warm temperature, the maples were bare and the oaks adorned with brittle brown remnants of last season's mantle.

Sarah's house was a pristinely kept stone cottage. It reminded me of an historically important house, like those in Williamsburg, only her house was actually lived in. Her furniture was antique colonial, mostly oiled cherry and walnut. Her walls were adorned with pictures of Virginia's founding fathers and Civil War generals, and of her family, which dated back to Revolutionary War days. The wall and ceiling were plaster, highlighted with broad crown and chair moldings.

As a child, I was never sure what Sarah thought of me, and I didn't like visiting her house. Reilly was always warning me to be careful not to spill or break something there. That is not to suggest that Sarah was prim or formal. Her rough edges were obvious to anyone who knew her, or tried to get to know her. She could drink, smoke, spit, and cuss when provoked, but what provoked her no one quite knew. At the age of seventy, she was still feisty, unpredictable, and a little intimidating.

But today, Sarah gave me a hug and looked at me through red, swollen eyes. She apologized for "acting like an old fool" at the funeral home, then offered me coffee. I considered asking her for a beer. Since leaving prison, I've taken to drinking beer to calm me or to help me sleep when the nightmares come. I thanked her and she hurried off to the kitchen.

She returned with a silver tray loaded with a china pot, two cups, and two saucers. The china could have belonged to Robert E. Lee. I listened a few minutes to Sarah spewing out unrelated statements about how unfair it was that Reilly was dead, what a bastard he was for dying so close to Christmas, and an impossible to parse complaint about not leaving a note before checking out.

After a few platitudes, I asked, "Do you believe Reilly killed himself?"

Sarah patted my hand, and responded in a strong southern accent. (She once told me, "When I was young, there was no Yankees around to pollute the language.") "I understand the question. You think someone killed him because Reilly was too upbeat of late to kill himself. The thought had crossed my mind, too. Honestly, there are people in this town who disliked him and have for a long time. Maybe someone disliked him enough to kill him, but I don't know who that someone would be."

I drank my coffee slowly, not because it was hot, but because I was afraid it might take the porcelain off my teeth. I considered asking again about the stories of Reilly cheating the local folks out of their money, but decided against the direct approach. "Why would anyone hate Reilly?" I asked cautiously.

Sarah stared at me for what seemed like the longest time. I believe that the longer a person thinks about an answer, the more likely the answer will be a lie or a sophistic version of the truth. Finally, she cleared her throat. "Tell me about prison."

The response puzzled me. My indictment, conviction, and incarceration were not subjects openly discussed in my mother's social circle. Yet, the stigma that comes with doing time spreads well beyond the prisoner. Family must deal with the humiliation, the gossip, and the guilt by association. In my mother's case, I had given her "social enemies" a reason to whisper. As she was dying, and even after I was cleared of all charges, she had a hard time forgiving me. For Sarah to mention it, especially now, was odd, even for her.

Sarah continued. "You were accused and convicted of something you didn't do. You've been set free now. Tell me if you feel vindicated, if you feel like your reputation has been restored."

I shook my head. "I'm a felon, a liar, and a cheat. I always will be."

"True. And no one cares that your wife left you, that you were disbarred, or that you lost three years of your life. Reilly has been accused of cheating the locals out of their money. That was over thirty years ago. Reilly denied it. But what difference does it make? A lot of folks who say bad things about him know the truth but will never admit to it. It's just easier to tell old stories, especially if telling the truth means admitting to a previous lie."

"So what happened?"

Sarah looked down and took a few short breaths. I braced myself for another tirade, but her voice was soft, with a touch of sadness. "Reilly got a record contract. He was singing country music then. He had a string of hits and everyone in town hovered around him like mosquitoes at a picnic. Oh, the town was nice to him. Then some of the local know-it-alls got the idea to build a recording studio here in Lyle. Reilly agreed he'd use it, and a few other up-and-coming singers made verbal commitments. But Reilly didn't have a financial interest in the studio and wouldn't have made any money if the business had been successful. Even so, the group promoted the studio using Reilly's name and suggested that Reilly had given a personal guarantee that it would succeed. Reilly was so naïve that he didn't grasp the risk involved in letting his name be used that way.

"Dozens of local folk invested their life savings into the venture. Mind you, it wasn't a large sum of money by any big city standard. All told, maybe it was a hundred thousand dollars. But remember, this was Lyle, and a few thousand dollars back then represented years of hard work and doing without. Then something happened. Reilly would never say what it was, but he suddenly left town and the music studio deal fell completely apart. The studio was never built. The money the investors paid for the land had been inflated by all the speculation, so the land couldn't be sold for close to the amount they paid for it. All the investors ended up with was a piece of property that wouldn't grow moss. They blamed Reilly, accusing him of running out on them and taking their money, but it was their own greed that undone them."

"But he had to have a reason to leave town."

"If he did, he didn't share it with me or anybody else."

I thought for a moment. "Why do you think he took the stage name C.C. Hollinger?"

"I wish I could help you," she said, then laughed. "The people who might know are the ones who lost the most in the studio deal."

"Enough to kill him?"

"These days, people kill for a lot less," she said with a sigh, "but I can't say I know anyone in this town bitter enough to shoot Reilly."

I knew some things about the people involved in the studio deal—most of them old men now. I wanted to ask Sarah more questions about them, but the weariness in Sarah's voice convinced me to change the subject.

"Reilly said he wanted to talk to me about my father," I said. "Why he left me and my mother, what kind of person he was, things like that."

Sarah looked at me with such empathy I thought she might cry. "He mentioned it to me. He said it was going to be one of the hardest things he ever did, but that you had a right to know."

"What did he mean?"

"I really don't know," she said shaking her head. "Reilly was such a private man. He had all his secrets locked up inside him." She wiped a tear from her cheek.

"If he had something he wanted to tell me, why would he kill himself?" I asked the question and immediately saw my flawed logic. The point I was trying to make was that Reilly had plans, a future. Of course, there was another possibility—that the burden of whatever he wanted to tell me was so great that he snapped.

Sarah shook her head. "I don't know, Shep." She looked away, then stood up. "Just a minute. I'll be right back."

I heard her climbing the stairs so I glanced over the police report the sheriff had given me. I skimmed the whole thing, then studied a diagram Deputy Tittle had drawn of the body. Reilly was shot while sitting on the couch in his study. He had an entrance wound just below the left nipple and an exit wound at the lower area of the right kidney. The bullet penetrated the heart. Reilly, I surmised, was dead before his head hit the cushion.

I read the report several times, before I found what had been gnawing at me. The gun was reported found in Reilly's right hand, but the entrance wound was on his left side. I extended my right index finger and stuck it against my chest, then turned my hand so that the tip of my finger pointed at my right kidney. The only way I could manage this feat was to turn my wrist at a right angle. Why would anyone, bent on killing himself, assume such an unlikely position? Given that Reilly was almost twice my age, I was not even sure he was flexible enough to perform the maneuver.

I heard Sarah coming down the stairs, so I put away the report. She sat next to me and opened an old photo album. "Reilly told me you'd been asking questions about your father for years. I encouraged him and your mother to answer you, but both of them said the past was best left alone. I think you have a right to know, because in lots of ways we are defined by events that shaped our ancestors. I was born to the children of ex-slave owners. To understand why I think things or react to things, I have to know about my parents and how they grew up. For me, it's easy because the past was discussed openly. But for you, the past is shrouded in secrecy. That's not fair. For the longest time, Reilly didn't see it that way and made me swear not to encourage you. If he'd known about these pictures, he would have taken them and burned 'em."

She carefully turned the pages, pointing to pictures of Reilly and my mother as they were growing up. She found a picture taken when I was a baby. My mother, my father, and my grandmother were all near a stream having a picnic. My father was holding me, smiling as if he loved me. I had never seen the photo before, and questions jumped into my head. Sarah showed me other pictures in which my father was in the background, looking sad or simply forgotten. As I got older, he seemed to be in fewer and fewer pictures. In the last picture of him, I was hugging him and his face was beaming. I believe he left the following year.

Sarah closed the album and hugged it to her chest. "I spoke with your father a few times, but mostly he kept to himself. I could tell he loved you, but something wasn't right between him and your mother. I don't really know much more than that. Reilly knew, and that's what he wanted to talk to you about. Maybe Billy or Doc can help you."

She put the album away. When I got up to leave, Sarah came to me, pressed her head against my shoulder, and sobbed. "With Reilly gone, I don't have anyone else," she said. "I can't stand the idea of him at that funeral home all made up to look like a freak. I want you to talk to Billy about Reilly's funeral. I'll be attending the town council meeting this morning. You can meet me afterwards."

I patted her. I agreed to talk to Billy about a funeral and report back to her at the council meeting. But as seemed to be happening a lot these days, my mind was really elsewhere.

Chapter 4

The Reverend Billy Tripp arrived in town when I was sixteen. He was about forty then, but he hasn't aged much since. Billy seemed likeable enough, but an unlikely man of the cloth, unless Friar Tuck is your model. For one thing, he liked to drink and bowl. His first sermon seemed more about throwing a good hook on an oily lane than it was about the Bible or the Lord. But the people in town liked him and still do.

I'm not particularly religious. I met a man in prison—his name was Jesse—who was the same way, but suggested I still treat the clergy with a certain deference: "Religion serves as a form of population control. More people have died in the name of one god or another than have died of any pestilence God himself may have visited upon the earth," he said. "But one faith might have gotten it right, so don't go out of your way to make any of them mad at you."

Jesse was a complex person in some ways. For every principle he espoused, he readily cited a competing one. While he preached deference to the clergy and to religion, he made it clear that a person should only take so much grief. The difference between Jesse and me was in the amount of grief each of us considered excessive. Jesse graduated to a maximum-security prison after he removed the ear from an inmate who teased him about being short. When it comes to tolerating other people, I practice what I call optimistic skepticism, meaning I want to believe people even though I think they're lying.

So I went to find the Reverend Billy Tripp to see what he knew about Reilly's death. I also wanted to know why in hell he wouldn't bury Reilly. Billy might have a reason—my mind was open—but I couldn't think of one that would appease me.

Billy's church—and the only church within the town limits—was located a few blocks from the center of town on the corner of Main Street and West Third Street. The church was a stone structure with a slate roof and a classic steeple adorned with a cross on which a large bird was perched. The bird looked to me to be a hawk, and I studied it as I walked. As I reached the corner, I saw a shape enter my peripheral vision, but it was too late to avoid colliding with it. I was instantly on my back on the sidewalk. A woman was lying on top of me. The woman scrambled to her feet and looked at me. She was about five-seven, athletic, and nicely proportioned in pants and cashmere sweater.

"I am so sorry," she said. I didn't move. "Are you hurt?" I looked into her eyes. "Are you all right?" she asked again, rather musically.

The owner of this songbird's voice was more than the sum of her components and more than the female form seen from a man's eye. Just looking at her made me lonely.

"Fine," I said, getting up. "I was daydreaming."

"Me, too. I'm Cali McBride," she said, offering her hand.

"Shep Harrington. Nice to meet you."

I saw a glimmer in her eye. "Maybe you can help me," she said. "I'm working on a story about Reilly Heartwood."

"You're a reporter?"

Cali nodded. "For the Valley Post."

"Have a nice day," I said and headed toward the church.

"You're that Harrington, the one who went to prison?" I didn't answer. "I did a story on you, about how you were falsely convicted."

I stopped. "Let me guess. My conviction ran on page two, and my release was a small note on page thirteen."

"I wrote it, but they didn't print it. But if I could interview you . . ."

"You can't, Ms. McBride. Besides, no one would read it."

"Well, they can't if no one writes it, now can they?"

She was spunky, all right. I turned again.

"Okay," she said, "could you just answer a few questions about Reilly? I'm tryin' to finish an assignment before Christmas. I could use some help."

I wanted to get away. For no fault of her own, Cali McBride made me think about things I'd lost—my wife, for one. Despite my misgivings, I approached her cautiously, as if she might bite if I got too close. "I'll help you with your story about Reilly, but you won't mention me directly or by implication."

Cali nodded. "All right."

"I'll meet you for lunch at Brown's. It's on Main Street."

"I'm sorry, but I have to get this done this morning. I just need a little information to finish an obituary."

"What do you know so far?"

"All the background stuff. Where he was born, where he went to school, about his music. What I need to get clear is what reason he'd have to kill himself."

"Maybe he didn't," I said. I was messing with her. Messing with reporters was actually a sport. "Have a reason, I mean. But we can ask some of his friends. Will that help?"

Cali nodded. "As long as it doesn't take too much time. I have to be in Winchester this afternoon."

I led Cali to the east side door of the church. Billy's office was to the right and downstairs. His door was open and I could hear his labored breathing before I saw him.

Billy was no taller than five-eight, but weighed close to two hundred and fifty pounds. Besides a belly that rivaled Santa's, he stored his mass in huge jowls, multiple chins, ham-sized arms and thighs. Exertion of any kind—even bowling—made him wheeze.

I found him pacing, apparently deep in thought. I knocked lightly on the jamb, startling him despite my intention not to. I expected a warm hello but received a look of terror.

"Shep? What are you doing here? Who's she?"

"I wanted to talk to you about Reilly. And this is Cali. She's my parole officer. Has to follow me wherever I go. She's very loyal and incredibly discreet."

Cali offered a hand. "Nice to meet you."

"You can't stay," said Billy. "I have an appointment." He tried to force a smile, but the effort produced only a grimace. "Maybe later."

"This won't take long," I said, motioning to Cali. "Cali wants to know why Reilly shot himself."

"Why would she want to know that?" asked Billy.

"I think she thinks I shot him."

Billy shook his head. "I have no idea why he took his life.

On the day he died, he agreed to meet with me the next day to discuss the residents of the poor farm. He seemed in good spirits."

"Was Reilly in any kind of trouble that you know of?" I asked. "You know, was anyone more pissed at him than usual?"

"Are you asking if I think someone killed him?" replied Billy.

Cali looked at me. "Reilly Heartwood was murdered?"

"Not officially," I said. Then I looked at Billy. "So why won't you bury him? He was your friend. He was a lousy bowler. Seems to me you could have him in the ground tomorrow."

Cali raised her hands in frustration. "You've lost me."

"You've got to stay focused," I said. "Officially, Reilly killed himself, but no one can say why. Also, Billy won't arrange his funeral for reasons he's about to explain. Now you're caught up."

A deep furrow crossed Billy's forehead. "She doesn't have to hear this."

"Sorry," I said, "but she blames me for everything. And she has ways of making me talk. It's just easier if we put all our cards on the table."

"I've got an appointment," said Billy. "Come back later."

I wasn't in the mood for later, but as I was about to say so, Billy's eyes moved to the doorway behind me. The three of us turned and saw Terry McAdams, the administrator of the poor farm, standing in the doorway. In contrast to Billy, Terry was tall and thin. He was also an excellent bowler who carried a two hundred plus average, a fact that sometimes drove lots of people in town—Billy for one—to irreverent thoughts.

"Hey, Shep. Billy."

I nodded and introduced Cali. "How's everything at the farm?"

"Good. Real good. The residents know you're in town. The twins have been talking about you a lot." Terry looked at the floor. Billy seemed to be staring at nothing.

"Is Rose with you?" asked Billy.

"No," said Terry. "She sent me to fetch you."

Billy sighed. "Is she in one of her moods?"

"You know Rose," said Terry.

"Is it bad?"

Terry nodded. "She's been carrying on about Reilly and how he took her house, that kind of thing, mostly when she hears the other residents talking about how they miss him. Last night, she started in on how the church owes her family, and that you better not let Reilly be buried in the church cemetery." Terry looked at me. "She also had some unkind things to say about your mother."

"Like what?" I interjected.

Again Billy cut in before Terry could answer. "Did she say anything about me?"

"Nothing specifically," replied Terry. "Just the usual stuff about the Abernathy family, how it was her people who'd settled this county and built this town, and she took some shots at Reilly and Mary. I guess I got her all riled up this morning when I refused to have her breakfast taken to the porch—the sun deck as she calls it. The woman still acts like she's the richest person in town. She's living on a poor farm, for Christ's sake. It really pisses me off." Terry looked at the floor. "Sorry about my language, Billy."

Billy grimaced. "She pisses me off too."

"What do you mean, poor farm?" asked Cali. "And who is Rose?"

"I'll explain later," I said. "At lunch."

"Hey, Shep," said Terry. "Why don't you and Cali come out to the farm with me? You can talk to the residents while Billy deals with Rose, and Cali can see the farm first hand. I'll drive you right back."

The fear returned to Billy's face, and I knew he was pleading with me not to go. The polite thing would have been to decline the invitation, but I was curious to find out what Rose was saying about my mother and why Billy was so terrified of her.

"I'd be happy to," I said, and was almost certain I heard Billy asking God to damn me. Cali seemed perplexed. "You'll like the farm," I said to her, "and the residents like meeting new people. Maybe Terry knows something about Reilly that will help you." She was teetering, so I added, "It's only ten now. You'll be back in an hour and still have time to cover the poinsettia festival this afternoon. I promise."

As we headed for the door, Cali said something about working on a story about a serial killer. And she was still expressing her concern about her afternoon appointment as we piled into Terry's car and headed out of town.

The poor farm was located a few miles to the north and west of Lyle, between the town and the interstate, off Rural Route 1200. The driveway was a dirt road marked by a break in a barbed wire fence and a large rusted mailbox sitting on a locust post. The post leaned back, but with the help of a labyrinth of

Virginia creeper and honeysuckle vines, managed to defy gravity. Up close, one could see the faded letters announcing this as the entrance to "FARM No. 38." But it had been a long time since anyone had been that close.

Terry turned onto the dirt road. Shadows cast by the naked maples lining the drive flickered against the windshield. I found myself remembering trips to the farm with Reilly and the anticipation of playing on the farm equipment and riding horses. Those days were light years ago, yet felt like they were just yesterday.

Terry glanced at Cali, who was riding in the front seat, then began his routine as tour guide. "The original farmhouse was a small stone building. It sported a dungeon that was used to punish runaway slaves, and, according to local legend, residents who broke the rules. Two dormitory wings were added during the Great Depression. Only one is in use now and, judging by the age of the five residents, the time is rapidly approaching when only the farmhouse will be needed."

"This is a state facility?" asked Cali.

"Not really. The land was leased to the state during the thirties. The lease expired years ago. Technically, this is a private facility operated by a corporation that I'm certain never realized the farm was on the books. Until now, anyway."

Terry pulled up a hundred yards from the house and stepped from the car. Billy, Cali, and I followed, uncertain what the problem was. Terry looked past us. "You know there's talk that the farm is going to be sold?"

Billy shrugged. "There are rumors like that every year."

Terry shook his head. "I was telling Cali that I didn't think the land owners knew they were paying for a boarding house. That's changed. I've seen a few blue suit types stomping around here, pointing at things, and looking at a plat. Even a lawyer or two among them. This time, it looks serious." Terry made a face, then spit. "When this many people are getting screwed, you can bet there's a lawyer involved somewhere. God damn lawyers." He winced, then looked at Billy.

"I don't like 'em either," said Billy.

I was waiting for a personal exception, but it never came.

"I think we've got to start planning what we're going to do with the residents if the property is sold," said Terry. He turned to me. "Maybe there's some legal move we can make while we figure something out, Shep. If we knew who's going to buy the place, we could rent the house—at least until the residents die. Or you could sue their asses until they give up."

It's funny how everyone hates lawyers until they need one. Even a disbarred lawyer like me is better than none at all.

"I'll think about it," I said.

Billy and I took a few steps toward the car, but Terry took Cali's elbow and walked her a few feet down the driveway. "Farms like this one were run to make life so miserable that only the desperate would come."

All my internal mechanisms searched frantically for a way to divert Terry from his favorite subject. Terry was writing a history of Farm No. 38 and had been since anyone could remember. He would talk endlessly about poor farms and there was no polite way of stopping him. "Well, I guess it didn't work on this farm," said Billy with a laugh.

"What do you mean?" asked Terry in a defensive tone.

"Oh, I was only kidding," replied Billy.

"The farms weren't a place for humor," responded Terry. "They were modeled after the workhouses the English set up in 1832. A person got food and shelter in return for sweat labor— none of this mailing a check to the poor stiff so he could go out and spend it. If he were too poor to fend for himself, well, the poor farm would mean he wouldn't starve. Or at least, that was the theory."

"Really?" said Billy. "I hadn't realized that. Perhaps I can work some of that history into a sermon someday."

I was sure Billy would soon regret saying so. "An excellent idea," said Terry. "My book will paint a pretty grim picture. Most of the folks who came to the farm were the old, the disabled, retarded people like Jamie, and real crazy people—not a great work force to be counting on. But that was a sign of success, you see. The theory was called scientific charity. You can't make the farm too nice or the able-bodied would show up. Yup, only the deadbeats could handle it, and that was taken as proof that the theory was right." Terry looked at Billy. "Course, the bureaucrats failed to figure out that by not paying these folks, they stayed poor and stuck around forever."

"Another excellent point," said Billy, walking toward the car. "Well, I guess I better get this over with," he added, still searching for a way to cut Terry off.

"Always best to get bad news behind you," said Terry, who, to my relief, was getting back into the car.

Billy, Cali, and I joined Terry as he pulled up in front of the house. Four residents were sitting on the porch taking advantage of the unseasonably warm air. I turned to Cali. "The men playing checkers are Cecil and Harry Drake. They're twins—they came to the farm as children after their parents died in a fire. They just showed up after the funeral and were taken in on a temporary basis, which meant until after harvest. They were good workers and stayed for every harvest since.

Next to them is Carrie Toliver, the only resident to have been born on the farm. She's at least eighty and hasn't set foot off the property in sixty years other than to attend my mother's funeral. Closest to the door is Jamie Wren. He doesn't say much, but he has a knack for writing offbeat sayings for fortune cookies and greeting cards that appeal to city folk. Each month, Terry sends his scribbles to an agent in New York. Jamie's most popular one-liner was, 'The next five minutes of your life may not be enough.' He also did well with, 'Misery loves company but doesn't deserve it.'"

"Who's Rose?" asked Cali.

"Rose is the last surviving member of Lyle's most prestigious family. Her father lost the family fortune twice while Rose was still in her teens. She never learned a skill to make money, at least not one that was legal. But she sure learned how to spend money. For awhile, she managed to hold on to her house through handouts from relatives, but all that ended some twenty years ago when she lost the house in a foreclosure sale to an unnamed buyer. The buyer turned out to be Reilly and that, as they say, is history. What happened to her after that is one of Lyle's secrets. All I know is that five years ago, Terry took her in as his guest, allowing her to deny that she was a resident of the poor farm. Apparently, Rose viewed this overture as a license to make the rest of the residents miserable."

As we approached the porch, Cecil, Harry, and Carrie were calling my name and making quite a fuss. Carrie was signing as well, an old habit left over from the days before Reilly arranged to have her fitted for hearing aids. I signed back "hello."

I have to admit I took great pleasure at the reception. I may have buried the touchy-feely part of me behind serious defenses, but we ex-felons don't often get such positive greetings. I wondered if Terry's concerns about the farm being sold were well founded. I couldn't imagine the residents living anywhere else. As the twins smothered me, I made a mental note to talk to Terry about it later.

Billy arrived huffing and puffing. "Hey, Jamie," said Billy, resting on the top step. "What's that you're working on?" To my surprise, Jamie handed him a pad. Repeatedly scrawled across it were the words, "Getting old is no excuse for not being young."

"Jamie's been kind of stuck on that one for a while," said Terry. "I don't think it's going to be a big seller, but the city people can surprise you. A few years ago, he made a bundle out of 'two's company but you're a crowd.' Just goes to show you what living in a big city can do to you, doesn't it?"

I introduced Cali, who suddenly became the center of attention. She smiled sweetly at the three lost souls competing for her attention. Billy stood to one side, his eyes focused on the door to the main house. The house was supposed to be the residence of Terry and his wife, Norma. Reluctantly, they had allowed Rose to take a room in it with them. The other residents had threatened to kill her or throw her in the dungeon if she remained in the dormitory. Billy smiled at us, mumbled something that might have been a prayer, and went inside.

A moment later, the door swung open and Billy's eyes locked on me. "Shep. Rose wants to speak with you."

"Me? About what?"

Billy struggled for words. "She wants an apology. She wants you to apologize for something Mary did."

Chapter 5

Rose was seated in a high-backed Victorian chair between two windows in the corner of the small living room. She sat erect, her gloved hands folded in her lap. From a distance, she cast the aura emitted by the prominent, favored people of God's flock, though she had long lost her claim to such status.

If Rose were trying to masquerade as the dame of the poor farm, the effort ran into serious trouble when the first whiff of gin hit me. It failed altogether when her haggard, defeated face came into focus. Ravaged by booze and bitter memories, she glowered at me through yellow eyes encircled by great bags of sagging, blue-white skin. Deep creases around the corners of her mouth pulled her lips into a downward arch. Just a few years past sixty, Rose wore the face of someone on the edge of death. That she was very much alive was potential evidence that God has His reasons for deciding who should live or die, or that God doesn't exist at all, or that both God and Satan are afraid of her and have conspired to keep her on earth as long as possible.

"Good morning, Rose," I said in the most friendly tone I could muster.

The muscles in Rose's face flexed like so many snakes writhing under a thin blanket. "Don't you good-morning me," she snarled. "You know God damn well this is not a good morning."

"I do now," I replied. "What ruined it for you?"

"You're Mary's boy all right. You certainly have her mouth." She nodded, agreeing with some unshared thought. "It didn't surprise me that you went to jail. Whatever your father's name, you've got Kilgore blood. Kilgores have always been scoundrels. Most of the time they manage to get away with their foul deeds. I can't deny that I took some pleasure in hearing that you didn't."

"I was taught that if you can make someone happy, you should go out of your way to do it," I said, understanding better why mother had hated Rose so much.

Rose ignored me. "And now Reilly's gone and shot himself."

"Maybe he had help," I replied.

A hint of a smile crossed Rose's face. "I dare say there would be no shortage of volunteers." She looked at Billy. "Enough of this small talk. The point is I know why Shet? Chet?..."

"Shep," offered Billy.

"... whatever. I know why he's in town." Rose's chest heaved. "The church and the cemetery are on land my grandfather donated. It's Abernathy land. And I will not let you bring Reilly's body into my church or bury him in my graveyard."

Billy wiped a small drop of spittle from his cheek. He avoided looking at me, as did Rose. I was in the room to hear the edict but not to comment on it. I waited for Billy to challenge her ownership of the church and its cemetery, but he said nothing.

"Rose," I said softly, "everyone deserves to die with dignity." I paused at this statement, wondering how committing suicide fit into this generality, then pressed on. "Reilly is entitled to a funeral. Perhaps you should put aside your animosity for a moment and let ..."

"Animosity? Is that what you call this?" She was shrieking. "Son, you spent too much time in prison if you think this is about some petty animosity." She leaned over, her face inches from mine. I held my breath to avoid secondary intoxication. "That man ruined me and my family. If it weren't for him, I'd be living in my house in the style to which I became accustomed and which I most certainly deserve."

I glared at Billy. I expected him to respond to this vile woman. I expected him to tell her that it wasn't her church or her cemetery, that she didn't own the town. I expected him to defend Reilly, to tell Rose that she was contemptible. I waited for him to say all of these things, but he said nothing.

I was deciding if I'd reached my limit of Rose's arrogance when she turned back to Billy. "I know you'll do the right thing."

"The right thing," repeated Billy.

Rose's face softened. Even some of the lines seemed to disappear, as if the exercise of power had revitalized her. "We all have a past, Reverend. Some of us are haunted by it. Some of us, like you, have risen above it. I think you know that resurrecting the past is far easier than burying it twice."

I'd heard enough. "What the hell is all this about, Billy? She doesn't own the God damned cemetery. Tell her."

"I can't Shep," he said meekly. "It's complicated."

"Complicated? That's supposed to excuse letting Reilly rot without a funeral? For Christ's sake, Billy, what's wrong with you?"

Billy looked away without answering.

The muscles in Rose's face rippled again, but she maintained her calm demeanor. "I don't want you to think of me without compassion," she said. "I am not so proud that I can't put aside my personal feelings—however justified—and allow Reilly to be put to rest in the church cemetery."

"I think you lost me," said Billy, echoing my thoughts.

"Putting aside the pain of what Reilly did to me would be easier," she said, "if I were rewarded with an act of contrition by someone who has wronged me."

"I don't think Reilly is in any shape to be acting contrite," said Billy.

Rose sighed impatiently. "I was thinking more of Shep."

"Shep?" asked Billy.

"I believe that Shep has the duty to offer an apology to me for his mother's behavior. Such an apology would have a very positive impact on me."

"Rose, all that happened before I came to Lyle," protested Billy.

The corners of Rose's mouth dropped suddenly. "It was yesterday, and the day before, and the day before that. I suffered assaults from that loathsome woman every day for twenty years. I waited for an apology, but she had the nerve to die before doing so." Rose's voice had become a hiss without tone or modulation. "No one, especially a Kilgore, treats an Abernathy that way. You and Billy let her ashes be sprinkled in my cemetery. Well, no more. No one gets buried there until I get an apology. I know you'll arrange it."

I touched Billy's arm. "What is she talking about?"

Billy pulled loose, then grabbed the back of the chair to steady himself. He was suddenly short of breath and his knees seemed to have trouble supporting his considerable weight. He looked at me, then stumbled past the residents and Terry. I heard the car door slam.

I turned to Rose, who by now was reveling in a victory I didn't understand. "I don't know what my mother may have done...."

"Talk to Sarah or Doc or Terry or Billy. They'll tell you."

"Right. And if I apologize for it, you'll allow Reilly to be buried?"

She nodded. "I will write down what I want you to say."

I detested this woman, but some battles aren't worth fighting. I had no idea what my mother could have done, but I didn't care. If an apology for some old sin would get Reilly in the ground, then so be it.

She turned her head, and I knew I had been dismissed.

The porch was buzzing with voices until I stepped outside. I felt all eyes on me. Then Terry stood in front of me. "You're not going to apologize to the old witch, are you? You're not going to betray Mary?"

I knew the right answer was "no," but I desperately wanted to say "yes." "I haven't decided to do anything."

"You should talk to Sarah," said Terry.

"Talk to Sarah," said Jamie, who repeated the words over and over.

"Good idea," I said, then headed for the car.

Nothing in Lyle was easy.

Chapter 6

The ride back from the poor farm was a quiet one. I tried to ask Billy about the apology, but all he could manage was "talk to Sarah." It was league night and Terry and Billy preferred talking about bowling. Cali and I exchanged glances, but said little. I think she was dying to ask me questions, but sensed that I was in no mood to answer them. As we arrived in town, I asked Terry to take Cali to her car, and to let me out on the pretext I was feeling carsick. I wasn't feeling ill. I just wanted to be by myself.

Cali slid toward the open door, but I closed it. She glared at me. "You better get back to work," I said. "You might miss a scoop on the meaning of Christmas."

Terry pulled away as I headed down the street. In a few minutes, I reached a familiar wrought-iron fence that surrounded the town cemetery. I glanced up the hill to the large oak towering above a marble obelisk placed in memory of the Kilgore family. Reilly had purchased the plot next to my mother's. It seemed a simple matter to dig a grave and bury Reilly. Yet, for reasons I couldn't fathom, Rose had chosen to exact a measure of revenge when it was too late to hurt either Reilly or my mother. I considered this for a moment, but still could not see the point of inconveniencing a dead person.

Two blocks from the cemetery, I came to the place where the

road was divided by an eight-foot square of concrete. The effect of the divider was to make the lanes on either side too narrow for most drivers. The metal fence that surrounded the divider had been hit from all sides, and the corner posts sagged toward the resulting wounds.

Inside the fence was a stone slab. Virginia creeper and poison ivy covered most of it. Even so, I could still make out the outline of a guitar and the first few words of "Lonesome Song" on one face of the slab. At the very top of the slab was the testimonial—"To C.C. Hollinger—For everything you've contributed—Thank You—the Town of Lyle." The inscription was inaccurate in that Reilly had recorded "Lonesome Song" under his given name, not his stage name. That Reilly's family name wasn't anywhere on the monument was testimony to the hard feelings his departure left behind. Even so, the monument was thought to be good for business. The person maybe loathed, but the money he draws is not. A nice Christmas thought.

I had promised Sarah I'd meet her at the council meeting, and I was late. The council meeting was held in a shoebox-shaped two-story building that housed not only the town council and the mayor's offices, but a courthouse and a library as well. Its stone facade and civil war cannon gave it an added element of quaintness. Buried in my memory was an image of a small black jockey statuette holding a lantern, but there was no sign of any such belittling icon now.

The council hearing room was packed. Chairs on both sides of the center aisle were full and people were standing two-deep along the walls. I spotted a space by a window and pushed my way toward it.

I caught a smile from Mayor Pete Carson. "Mr. Harrington," said the Mayor. "Welcome to Lyle. Sorry about the circumstances."

Heads turned in my direction.

"Thank you, Mr. Mayor," I said.

The space was open because it was next to a radiator pushing out heat as if winter had actually arrived. I searched the crowd for Sarah Mosby, then searched it again, this time more carefully. I found her sitting at the council table, waving at me. I didn't know she'd been elected to the council and couldn't imagine how she could have managed more than a handful of votes. Sarah, like Lyle, was full of surprises.

"Do you have something to say, Sarah?" asked the Mayor.

"Not yet, but if you keep talking, I'm sure I'll think of something."

"All right," said Pete, "before we get to what everyone is here for, the next item on the agenda is the master plan." He turned on a projector, and a large map of the county appeared on a screen behind the council members. Areas were shown in colors corresponding to zoning codes described in a legend at the lower left corner of the screen. "We've discussed this for the last few weeks," continued Pete, "so I don't see the point of debating it again. All in favor?"

"Excuse me, Mr. Mayor," I said. Again, heads turned. "I'm sorry, but it seems there's a mistake on your map. You've got the poor farm zoned as commercial and residential. I'm sure that's a misprint."

"It's not a misprint," replied Pete. "It's called planning. We don't want to have to do this again, so we've broadened the zoning there to commercial and multi-family residential."

"But you've included the poor farm."

Suddenly, a young man stood. He was wearing an expensive pinstriped suit, a white shirt with dark striped tie, and cuff links: a lawyer's costume if ever there was one. I know because I once had a closet full of them. "I'm Tom Stewart. I don't believe the gentleman is a resident of Lyle or the county. For that reason, he doesn't have standing to raise a question about the master plan before the council."

I gave Squire Tom a "you're an asshole" smile, then said, "What Mr. Stewart is saying in legal speak, Mayor, is that zoning of the poor farm is none of my business."

The room echoed with laughter. Laughing at a lawyer is a sport for the whole family.

"Thanks for that translation, Shep."

I wasn't done. "But I'm curious if there's an agenda for the poor farm that you forgot to mention during your deliberations."

The silence was as sharp as the look Squire Tom shot back at me. The Mayor covered his microphone and whispered something to the councilman to his right.

"There's no agenda, Shep. We've included lots of farms in the new zoning plan. Anyone wanting to use the land for something other than its current use would have to apply for a permit and the board of zoning review would have to agree to it."

"This discussion is pointless and unnecessary," said Tom. "The council should vote, and move on to the next issue."

Sarah started to speak, but the Mayor smacked his gavel and forced a vote. The motion passed eight to one, with Sarah the lone dissenter.

The Mayor cleared his throat. "The last matter on the agenda was brought to the council by Councilman Drexel Seymour." The eyes swung to the opposite end of the council table to a man wearing a bow tie and round wire-rimmed glasses. He met the collective gaze by pushing back the boyish lock of hair that fell across his forehead. I knew him as a partner in one of DC's big-name law firms and from law school.

"Councilman Seymour has proposed, again, the removal of the divider from Main Street," said the Mayor. "All in favor?"

Sarah jumped up from her seat. "Wait a God damn minute," she screamed. "My brother just died. And whatever you might think of Reilly Heartwood, that monument is the only tourist attraction this town has. People are going to come visit his grave. We shouldn't tear the monument down. We should remove the weeds and fix it up nice."

A man in the audience stood up. "You can't drive around the damn thing without tearing up your tires."

"If you didn't drink in the middle of the day, you might be able to drive in a straight line," countered Sarah.

"Reilly chose, Ms. Mosby, to take his own life, " said Councilman Seymour. "Whatever he may have contributed to Lyle, it's time to move on. Personally, I don't believe we want Lyle to be remembered for this man."

Chester Atkins rose from the audience and stepped into the aisle. He was about ten years older than Reilly, making him around seventy. He was tall and thin and his hands shook slightly, giving the appearance of being frail and meek. Chester was neither.

As I understood the story he, along with Larry Owens, came up with the idea for the music studio, formed a consortium, bought the land, and sold shares, all based on Reilly's word that he'd use the studio exclusively after it was built. Before the studio deal collapsed, Chester was on his way to being a wealthy man in the county. He had accumulated various properties and had opened the county's first bowling alley. After Reilly left town, Chester lost most of his holdings. Today, he works as the salaried manager of the bowling alley he once owned.

The only time I heard Reilly speak of Chester was when Reilly and I encountered him on a walk. Chester saw Reilly and began shaking like a frightened dog, only Chester was pissed, not scared. As Chester crossed the street to avoid us, Reilly said, "Poor Chester. Poor, poor Chester." I didn't know what it meant at the time and don't even now. In truth, I don't have a lot of empathy for people like Chester.

Chester cleared his throat. "You all have known me for years," he said softly, "and I think Mr. Seymour's got a point. Reilly Heartwood was as vile a man as there was. I invested everything I had in his music studio and a lot of other folks did too." His voice grew louder and was tinged with bitterness. "He knew we was relying on him. But he left us holding the bag." Chester began breathing harder. "I had three top names signed to recording contracts," he said, pounding his fist into his palm. "If he'd waited six months, he could've left town and it wouldn't have made no difference. But for the grace of God Almighty, a lot of us could have joined Rose at the poor farm because of that man. He's pond scum."

"We know all about that, Chester," said Pete, "and we're all sorry."

"Then get that God damned thing out of the street!" Chester shouted.

"Chester Atkins tells a sad story," said Sarah. "'Course, he doesn't mention that he and his friends were using Reilly's name to bring in other singers and that Reilly got nothing from the studio. I think the Mayor's forgotten that without Reilly, this town wouldn't be visited at all. And Mr. Seymour, like most carpetbaggers, likes to have opinions about things he doesn't know a hoot about. Saying Reilly cheated people doesn't make it so."

Chester threw his chair into the aisle. "The son-of-a-bitch ruined the lives of a lotta people in this room twenty years ago and he did it again last week. The land we bought back then for the studio—we had an opportunity to sell it this time to a developer. There would've been money for our kids and grandkids, paying our medical bills, having something to retire on. Reilly wouldn't agree to the deal . . ."

Squire Tom jumped from his chair. "That's enough, Chester."

"It's not enough. People here should know that Reilly could have made our lives better, could have made amends but chose not to. All he had to do was to agree to sell the poor farm and the deal was done. But he didn't. Now the developer will move the project up the road and we'll get nothin' again. Reilly deserves to be dead and he deserves to go to hell. If you don't remove that damn memorial, I'll do it myself and I'll have plenty of help."

I'd heard enough. "What's with you people? You say that Reilly cheated you and deserves to be dead. Well, who in this room knew that Reilly owned the poor farm? I didn't, although it doesn't surprise me. In a very quiet way, Reilly was a generous man to people in need. That you aren't driving BMWs isn't what I'd call a tragedy."

The room buzzed with voices. I managed to discern a few unflattering words directed at my heritage. It took ten gavel bangings to quiet everyone.

"I got one more thing to say," said Chester. "Sarah owns the farm now. So tell us. What are you going to do to make this right?"

The room was quiet, waiting for Sarah to answer. But the silence was broken by a voice from the back of the room. I turned and saw Robbie standing on a chair. "Sarah does not own the poor farm," she said. "Reilly's will leaves the farm to Shep Harrington."

Words can be powerful missiles. For me, the words "we find the defendant guilty" arrested the hands of time. Robbie's announcement of my inheritance took my breath away. All eyes were suddenly upon me. I held back a smile. Fate was jerking Lyle's poor, pathetic people around and they deserved it. I suppressed my bemusement as I tried to think of something to say. Then Chester said it for me.

"So now our future depends on a God damned ex-convict?"

I couldn't have said it better myself. The room again was filled with a chorus of angry voices. Christmas in Lyle is an experience I will never forget.

"That's enough," said Pete. "Do you have anything to say, Shep?"

I did, but most of it was irrelevant. "I will defer to what

Reilly wanted," I said. I'm a status quo kind of person until I'm convinced the status quo needs changing.

Chester gave me a cold look, then turned and headed for the door. Moments later, the room began to empty.

Pete rapped his gavel a few times, but the exodus continued. "The other members of the council and I have come to the conclusion that the amount of money that the memorial to C.C. Hollinger brings in doesn't justify having the bloody street split in two."

"Next time you boys decide something at the urinals, invite me in," said Sarah. "Anyway, you can't vote on an expenditure of funds until you know how much it's going to cost, and how much you're going to lose."

"Very well. All in favor of removing the Hollinger monument, pending an estimate and a final vote next week, say 'Aye'." Pete counted the hands, then nodded. "That's passed." The Mayor's pronouncement closing the meeting was barely audible over the sliding of chairs and grumbling of voices.

Sarah found me by the window and commented, "I had no idea Reilly owned the poor farm. I can't imagine him agreeing to sell it."

Tom Stewart approached me, walking now as if he were a male model. Before he spoke, he buttoned his suit jacket. "No hard feelings," he said, offering me his hand. I shook it politely.

"Not yet," I said. "And what exactly is your connection to all this?"

"I represent Mr. Atkins and others who held their shares in the studio land," said Tom. "We have an opportunity to realize a substantial gain on the current value of that property, contingent in a rather Byzantine way on the sale of the poor farm. I was discussing this with Reilly before he died."

What Tom had said in legal speak was that he had a deal—that's the meaning of "we"—that involved Tom packaging the studio land with the poor farm and making a killing. "Probably too complicated for me to grasp," I said shaking my head.

To my surprise, Amy Stewart joined us. I recognized her as the woman the deputy had been talking to outside the sheriff's office. She had large round eyes and a small expressionless mouth. She looked at me, and for a moment I thought she might be blind. I had seen eyes like hers in prisoners who were on drugs.

Amy blinked and her focus returned. We introduced ourselves, then she turned to her husband and said, "Hello . . . Tom. Sorry that you and your friends won't be buying the poor farm."

Tom hissed back. "Not here, Amy."

Amy had embarrassed Tom in front of the new owner of the poor farm. I tried to look at Tom in a new light, but he still looked like a snake. Then I looked at Amy, her V-neck sweater showing significant cleavage—something missing from my life for a few years.

"I'm an accountant," Amy said, "and I do estate work. If you or Sarah need some help with Reilly's estate, I'd be happy to pitch in. I worked with Robbie on the preliminary accounting, so I'm familiar with some of his assets."

Amy looked at me in a beguiling way. She wasn't exactly smiling, but her expression wasn't totally aloof, either. I was working on some twisted comment about "assets" but managed to suppress the impulse.

"Well, that'll make things easier if Sarah has questions."

Amy handed me her card, letting her fingers linger on my hand for a moment, then turned and left. The hand thing was for Tom's benefit, not mine. Tom didn't show any reaction other than to hand me his card. "We need to talk about the poor farm," he said as he departed. "I hope you're more reasonable than Reilly."

From the other side of the room, I saw Robbie approaching me. "I wish you'd have let me explain about Reilly's will this morning," she said. She looked at me, then asked, "Are you feeling all right?"

"I'm fine." The heat from the radiator had tired me and brought on a throbbing headache. "I've never inherited a poor farm before. Kind of entertaining."

Robbie sighed. "Well, then you should be more entertained when I explain the rest of the will to you."

Chapter 7

I had agreed to meet Robbie at her office in half an hour, but I needed caffeine in a major way. Fortunately, Lyle has a coffee boutique. I ordered a large mocha double espresso and stepped outside to a table bolted to the sidewalk. To my surprise, Amy appeared.

"I'm very sorry about your loss," she said. "I've been told that Reilly thought the world of you." Again the glassy eyes. I had little doubt that she was medicated. "Death is a horrible thing to deal with," she said. "And yet it happens every day." She looked away. "Worse, it's supposed to happen." Looking back at me, she said, "Do you think humans are the only animal that knows that? Of course we are. But we are still so very cruel to each other. I don't understand people sometimes."

I tried to look in her eyes, but she avoided my gaze. "Some deaths happen because of natural events," I said. "A bullet to the heart is different."

"Yes," she said, still averting her eyes, "I see that. You think Reilly was murdered. I can't imagine how that makes you feel. I mean, I would have a hard time believing that someone I cared for was killed. What are you going to do about it?"

The question was asked in a demanding tone that surprised me. "Do about it? There isn't much I can do. The evidence has been destroyed. The death certificate will be issued shortly. The sheriff says the case is closed."

"But you're not done with it. I can tell." Her tone was insistent, almost arrogant.

"Well, maybe. So far, I have a lot of questions and no answers," I said.

She sat down opposite me. "I'm sorry about what Tom and Mr. Atkins said at the meeting. You shouldn't have had to hear their ugly words." Her face went blank for a moment. "It's all about money. Men are obsessed with it. They think it brings them power. They confuse power with freedom. You understand the value of freedom, I'm sure." She lost focus again, then said: "I'd like to understand what it was like to be locked up, and how you dealt with it."

"I'm still dealing with it," I said, avoiding the subject.

Amy nodded. "Yes. I see that." She traced the pattern of the wrought iron table with her finger. "Reilly was a nice man. I spoke with him once. He really wanted to do the right thing with the poor farm. He thought the old people at the poor farm were more important than money. Tom and his clients couldn't understand that. They still don't. I understood what Reilly wanted. Do you?"

I sensed that Amy was probing me, but I had no idea for what. "Reilly had money," I said. "Maybe it was easy for him."

"Money doesn't make it easy for anyone. Tom was a very kind and gentle person when I met him. When we moved, we weren't poor, but we weren't rich either. And we had plans and dreams." She closed her eyes and moved her head slowly from side to side, as if someone were messaging her neck. "Beautiful dreams," she said sighing. A tear ran down her cheek, but she ignored it.

Looking at me again, she continued, "Tom joined a firm that did real estate deals. He got caught up in the game, chasing the big deal, and it changed him. Now he doesn't care who gets hurt by his deals. He just wants to close them. He doesn't care about anything but winning, and he'll do anything to win. He wasn't very nice to Reilly. He pressed him really hard to change his mind about the poor farm. He won't be nice to you."

I was certain that Tom wasn't always nice to Amy either. On the other hand, my instincts told me that living with Amy was no party. She stood up, her eyes regaining their distant look, then walked away. I sat for a moment and tried to grasp what Amy was trying to say, but could make no sense of it.

જૂ

Robbie's office was one of the renovated townhouses in the northeast section of town. Her foyer was small but inviting. Just inside and along the front of the room were a love seat and two matching chairs. To the left, her door was marked in bold letters: "Roberta L. Babcock, Attorney." Babcock is Robbie's married name. The receptionist's desk was just past the door, but it was unattended.

The office had a genuinely warm feel to it. The back of the room opened to a small patio. Light flooded the room through a set of French doors. Plants hung everywhere, adding color to the room and the fragrance of humus to the air.

I took a seat in front of her desk. She joined me a few minutes later with two cups of coffee and a platter of cookies. "I've still got a sweet tooth," she said smiling.

I caught her looking into my eyes and wondered if she were toying with my affections. I gave her my best lonely-guy look, but she reached for a large oatmeal raisin cookie and ignored me.

We sat quietly for a moment, then she said, "You look good."

"You mean, for someone who just got out of jail?"

"Yeah, something like that. It must have been awful." Another moment of silence passed. "And how is Anna?"

"She divorced me soon after I began serving my sentence. She didn't want to be sitting around for twelve years waiting for my parole. Can't blame her, really. I believe she's seeing someone, but I'm not sure."

I thought I was getting the right signals this time, when she added, "You should too. I know it's hard to get back into a personal relationship. But take it from me, you can care for someone again."

"Thanks," I said. "You don't know how much it means to me to hear you say that."

"Have you thought about applying for reinstatement to the bar?"

I shook my head. "I haven't thought that much about the future. Honestly, I'm still working through things. I got a partial payout of a settlement with my old company. I've spent most of the money, and the company attorney for my old employer is holding back on paying the rest. So I may have to think about getting a job of some kind. I'm not sure if anyone will hire me ..."

I stopped talking because Robbie was smiling. "What?" I asked.

"Nothing," she replied, fighting a grin that was making her mouth twitch. "You were saying?"

I shrugged. "I'm done," I said, still uncertain what had struck her as amusing.

Robbie reached into one of those large briefcases trial lawyers use, and removed a folder. "We should get started," she said formally.

"I'm sure you know all this, but as Reilly's attorney, I'm compelled to explain it to you anyway. Sarah is the executor of his estate and is in charge of managing his assets until his will is probated and his assets distributed. I've already had an accounting done of his property and have some information about his bank accounts and stock holdings."

"What did the accounting turn up?"

Robbie gave me a puzzled look. "It's all in order, except for the assets related to his singing career and the two life insurance policies he purchased a little less than two years ago. The latter included the usual language denying benefits for death resulting from suicide within the first two years. But that's got nothing to do with you. Jeb Garrett, an attorney in Front Royal, managed his corporate accounts. He won't release Reilly's files until we provide him a death certificate and Sarah qualifies as the executor of the estate. That shouldn't take too long if I can ever get Sarah to go to the courthouse. She says she's busy, but I think she's just not accepting what's happened."

I thought for a moment. "Did you mean to say that the anniversary date of the insurance policies was coming up?"

"Next week. Why?"

I shrugged. "Nothing. Just seems odd that Reilly would leave insurance proceeds to someone, then kill himself before the policies would pay out."

"I hadn't thought of that," said Robbie. "The policies were to be paid to Frieda and Lora Jean Brady. He cared a lot for them."

"Who's Lora Jean?"

"A stray kid whose mother went to rehab and father went to jail. Lora Jean stayed with Reilly and helped Frieda part-time with Reilly's housework. Nice girl."

"I gather Tom represents Chester Atkins and some of the locals in a deal for the old studio property."

"That's right."

"Do you know whether he has a financial interest in the deal?"

"Not really. What are you driving at?"

I shrugged. "The meeting was like watching a soap for the first time. Just trying to figure out who the players are, that's all."

Robbie accepted the lie and turned to the papers on her desk. My prison-instinct kicked in again, this time about why Amy was so interested in Reilly's estate that she would volunteer to help Robbie do an accounting of it.

"Here's the bottom line. Reilly left Sarah a tidy sum that'll last her the rest of her days, and he left you the farm and the house and the bulk of his estate, including the rights to his music and other business interests. I don't have the final numbers, but Reilly had accumulated several million dollars and is probably worth ten times that amount."

Robbie had gotten my attention, but her words didn't fully compute. "I don't understand."

"You're a multi-millionaire," she said laughing.

"But why? Did he say why?"

Robbie shook her head. "He said he was going to write a letter explaining everything, but I guess he didn't get around to it. He discussed the will with Sarah so you don't have to worry about her."

I rubbed my temples. My head was pounding. I needed a beer. "This doesn't make any sense."

"The will needs to go through probate, but once Sarah is qualified as the executor, she can make a distribution to you at any time."

I thought for a moment. "What about the poor farm? Do I have to take it?"

"No. The executor can do what is necessary to protect the assets, so Sarah could sell the farm, or buy it from the estate and give you the money. I'd advise her that she should have something from you in writing."

Robbie produced a bottle of aspirin from her desk. I swallowed four of them with cold coffee, then asked, "Do you believe Reilly killed himself?"

Robbie leaned back in her chair. "Reilly was moody. He'd suffered a mild stroke and was fearful of having a major stroke that would leave him a vegetable. But lately, he was upbeat. Even after he broke his foot, all he could talk about was getting better, getting things done. He was a lousy patient, mind you, but he wasn't suicidal. He insisted that I make certain he was never a vegetable, but he wasn't living scared. He was very excited about your coming for Christmas. He told me he was going to make it right for everyone who hated him, even if he'd never intentionally hurt anyone in the first place."

I heard her voice catch, and she pursed her lips. She said, "I understand that. All I ever heard growing up was how Reilly ruined the studio deal that Chester and my father had put together. I was expected to hate Reilly, too, but when you were in town and I was around him, he was always nice to me. When I was about to graduate from high school, Reilly offered to help me with college.

"Not too long ago, I asked Reilly about the studio deal, but he wouldn't talk about it. He said that he had no right to contradict what my father had told me. But Reilly paid my tuition to school and then law school. And when Dad got sick and died, Reilly paid the bills. Anonymously, of course. He made me promise I'd never tell anyone. That's the way Reilly was."

I considered this for a moment. If he helped Robbie's father, who else had he helped?

"I can't believe he's dead," continued Robbie. "Like you, it's hard to accept the fact that he killed himself. But that's how suicide is. And Christmas is a very emotional time for some people."

"Do you think he was going to sell the farm?"

"I have no idea. He called a meeting at his house the night he died because he had some news. Maybe he changed his mind. But because nobody showed up, we'll never know."

"I think someone showed up," I said.

She looked into my eyes again, but this time I interpreted

the gesture as concern. "You've just inherited a fortune. You are free to do with it whatever you want. Have you considered that if Reilly were murdered because he wouldn't sell the poor farm, that the person or persons who did it might decide to kill you for the same reason?"

I hadn't. I was too busy trying to understand why Reilly named me as his principal heir.

Chapter 8

My mind was full, but my stomach wasn't. I headed for Brown's Chinese and American Cafe. When I stepped inside, I found Cali at a table. She was smiling at me, a dangerous signal coming from a reporter. "I'm not the serial killer," I said, sitting down. "But if you want to talk plea bargain, I'm sure I'm guilty of something. I thought you left town."

"I was going to, but I decided to drop in on the council meeting. Then I got to thinking. Serial killer stories are a dime a dozen. I mean, how many people outside this state care about someone who crushes skulls for a hobby? But a story about a famous recording artist, a town that won't bury him, a poor farm with some sweet forgotten people, and the hint of foul play, now that's got *Rolling Stone* written all over it. Then throw in an attorney who once was the poster boy for government fraud, and this story will rock. Which brings me to my first question: How does it feel to own a poor farm?"

I found Cali's smugness attractive in an irritating way. She was right, too. Reilly's story would make good copy. But I wasn't interested in being drawn into the public eye. "I'll help you," I said, "but only if I'm not part of the story. I don't want to be quoted, either."

"If I like the food, I won't quote you. But you are part of the story. I'll have to think about that."

I said, "Since we're talking about prying into the private lives of so many people, what are you running away from?"

"Excuse me?"

"You're too old for this to be your first job. And you don't seem like the type to be happy doing obits for a small town paper. My guess is that you got yourself exiled to Front Royal. You're looking for a ticket back to what you think is the real world."

"You think too much," she said picking up the menu.

Cali studied the menu, but I told her not to bother. "Phil Brown, the owner, was the only person besides my attorney and the FBI to visit me in prison. He'll take care of us."

I flagged down a waiter and asked for Phil. Then I noticed Tom and Amy Stewart. Tom's back was toward me, but I could see he was reading a legal brief and shaking his head. I couldn't see the papers, but, judging from his reaction, guessed they were from Amy's attorney. While Tom tried to determine the cost of becoming single, Amy, who was facing me, was ignoring him, her eyes flittering from me to some thing or place she was obviously not interested in.

A dark-haired man with a full beard appeared, then broke into a broad grin. "God damn if it ain't J. Shepard himself. How you be? I heard you was in town. Sorry to hear about old Reilly. I liked the dude, and his music was sweet."

He looked at Cali. "And who is this?"

I introduced Cali. Phil immediately started hitting on her, and I kept mum until I thought Cali was sufficiently offended, then asked, "So what's in the wok?"

"Chicken with cashews is recommended," said Phil. "It's also all there is."

"We'll have that and some of your hot and sour soup," I said. "And don't scrimp on the peppers."

"You got it, man. Fix you right up."

"He likes you," I said. "Did he drool on your sweater?" I didn't wait for an answer, but handed Cali the police report of Reilly's death. "You might want to read this," I said.

Cali made various faces while reading the one page report.

"Is this it?"

"That's it."

"I'm no expert on police reports, but this strikes me as less a statement of facts than a rationalization for a desired conclusion. I mean, Reilly is described as 'holding the weapon used to inflict the fatal shot in a manner consistent with suicide.' But the position of the weapon, what hand it was in, where his hand was—none of that is stated. All we know for sure is that the sheriff reported his arrival time at Reilly's house as 7:45, the weapon had four live rounds and one empty casing, and the gun was identified as 'unregistered.' We don't even know for sure that the gun belonged to Reilly. No one seems to have asked. I can see why you might be suspicious."

I put the police report in my pocket. Phil arrived with soup and noodles, rice, and a large helping of stir-fried chicken. We devoured it while Phil stroked his beard and babbled on about people I didn't know and things he was going to do when he "got his shit together." Fact of the matter was, all the scientists in Los Alamos couldn't get Phil's shit together. He took my appetite as a compliment, then decided to make Cali and me a cup of his special coffee. He cleared the table and scurried back to the kitchen.

I had forgotten about Tom and Amy, but then they appeared together at my table. Tom sat down, much to Amy's annoyance and mine. He glanced at Cali, then said, "I like coming to the point, Mr. Harrington. I want to know if you and I can do business."

I wiped my mouth with my napkin. "I like coming to the point, too, Mr. Stewart. I want to know which of your clients killed Reilly Heartwood."

My response stunned Tom for a moment. "Honestly, that's not my problem," he said.

"For God's sake, Tom, give it a rest," pleaded Amy.

"Shut up, Amy," snapped Tom, who then turned to me. "My clients offered Reilly an opportunity to sell a not very valuable piece of land at a decent price. He turned it down. If he'd lived, that would have been the end of it. But Reilly's dead, and now it's a whole new game. It's up to you. You can make a business decision that serves everyone a lot better."

"Are you asking a question or describing a motive for murder?" I asked.

"What about the residents of the farm?" asked Cali.

"What about them?" responded Tom. "This town and the county need jobs, tax revenue, and infrastructure improvements. It may sound insensitive, but I can't see letting four people who never contributed one thing to society stand in the way of this community getting what it needs."

"Or coming between a lawyer and his fee?" I interjected.

"I create wealth. I take a share. That's the society we live in."

I started to speak, but Tom cut me off. "The point here, Mr. Harrington, is that Reilly had his reasons for not selling the farm. Maybe he believed it was morally wrong to displace those old people. Maybe he was just being vindictive toward my clients. I don't know, and I don't care. He's dead. The decision is now yours, and you can make a reasoned choice. Do the right thing and sell the farm."

I gave Tom my best smirk. "Or what? End up dead?"

Tom laughed. "I don't care how you end up, Mr. Harrington, if you sell me the farm before you go."

I considered the words that came from Tom's mouth and wondered how he would have dealt with Reilly. Reilly was not a patient man. Tom would have worn on him quickly, and Reilly would have spoken his mind. I doubt Tom would have taken kindly to being told to fuck off. I wondered if he could be provoked into shooting someone.

Amy was fuming and tugging on Tom's elbow. He jerked out of her grasp, then stood up. "We'll talk later. If you ever want to see top dollar for the poor farm, you need me, Mr. Harrington. But the longer you wait, the lower the price." He tossed his business card onto the table, then left. The gesture was for effect—I already had one of his cards. But the arrogance of the act sealed my impression of him.

"Tell me you weren't like that before you went to jail," said Cali.

"Me? No way. He's much more empathetic."

Phil arrived with two small cups of dark coffee and a small plate of cookies. "Fortune cookies fresh from New York," he said. "Jamie from the poor farm writes for them. I can't believe this weird stuff really sells. I guess you got to go to college or something 'cause I just don't get it."

I pointed to the fortune cookies. "You pick," I said.

Cali took a cookie and cracked it, and I took the other.

"I'm sorry if you want me to apologize," said Cali. What does yours say?"

"Knowing isn't everything."

Chapter 9

The food recharged me. More than likely, it was Phil's high-test coffee sludge. It could raise the dead. Maybe I should give some to Reilly and ask him how he died.

Cali left peeved that I was holding back on her. I insisted I wasn't, but my voice made it clear I was lying. I hadn't talked to her in detail about the angle of entry and exit wounds or what I thought it might mean. I had no reason to trust her and every reason to want her to pester me. I watched her drive off, then headed to the Eternal Peace Funeral Home to speak with Jason Grubbs.

I was a half block from the funeral home when I first noticed the traffic. Cars were parked in crosswalks and on lawns where "PARK HERE-$5.00" signs had been posted. The license plates said these weren't local folks. I spotted an Alaska plate and one from Arizona. Deputy Tittle was trying unsuccessfully to direct traffic and stare at female drivers at the same time.

The sidewalk was jammed with people. I followed the line up the porch stairs to the front door. As I wedged my way forward, I heard protests from the crowd. A woman at the door held another sign that read: "Next Viewing —15 Minutes." She gave me a severe look. "Sir, you're going to have to stand in line like everyone else."

"You must be Mrs. Grubbs. My name is Shep Harrington."

"I don't care if you're St. Peter, you'll put your butt back on the sidewalk and wait like everyone else."

I could feel my patience drain away. I pushed by her, through the heavy drapes, and into the small chapel where Reilly's casket was on display. The room was full of people, all listening to a recording of Reilly singing a song of melancholy and lost love. Jason was standing to one side of the coffin, his face a mask of sorrow. "Could I speak with you?" I asked softly.

"Can it wait?" asked Jason. "This is a very somber moment. Besides, I think I'm on to something."

I grabbed Jason by the throat and pushed him against the wall. "Listen to me, you little worm. If you don't get rid of these people, close this casket, and start treating the dead with a little respect, you're going to join Reilly on the other side. But not before I disembowel you."

I loosened my grip and Jason stared back at me unmoved. "Well, aren't we the proper and pious one? So, how much do you want? Ten percent?"

"I'm not amused."

"Do I detect the voice of greed?" Jason laughed. "Well, it's almost Christmas, isn't it? Okay, thirty percent of net is my top offer."

"I have a better idea," I said calmly. "Reilly's remains belong to his estate. I want them delivered to his house this afternoon. I'll have his lawyer draw up the papers if you want."

"And if I don't?" challenged Jason.

"I'm sure when you and your lovely wife go to your little trade gathering, you won't want a video of this side show to precede you," I responded. "And I could always get an injunction and sue you for damages." That was lawyer BS, but most people believe lawyers can sue and enjoin anything.

"You wouldn't!" huffed Jason. He saw the answer in my face. "What about these people? His fans. What about them?"

I thought for a moment. "Tell them there will be a proper viewing for Reilly day after tomorrow starting at ten at his house. No charge."

As I left, I heard Jason trying to clear the room. I heard the crowd chant "refund, refund" and Jason pleading in a shrill voice not to hurt him. I made a mental note to tell Frieda to expect a little company.

On the way back to Reilly's house, I stopped and bought a six-pack of beer and a tin of salted peanuts. I stepped inside the house and found a tall, skinny girl, about fifteen, with sloping shoulders and a pout that looked permanent. She was sitting on the steps to the second floor, next to a pile of tissues, talking on a cordless phone. I heard "shut up" and "no way" several times as I made my way to the kitchen.

She got off the phone and looked at me through swollen eyes. You didn't have to be a doctor to see that she wasn't well. "Who might you be?" I asked.

"Lora Jean. You're Shep, right?"

"I am. So what do you do around here, LJ?"

"Feed the cats. Study. Whatever Frieda needs."

Frieda appeared and placed a hand on LJ's forehead. "I've called Doc and he's on the way over. I want you to lie down and stay off the phone."

"By the way," I chimed in, "where might I find a bottle

opener?"

"In the drawer next to the fridge." She looked at me hard. "Isn't it a bit early to be drinking?"

I didn't like the question, but I understood it. After my release from prison, I had gotten sloppy drunk while visiting Reilly, raising concerns I might be an alcoholic. No number of denials seemed to satisfy Frieda. The truth was that a beer or two let me sleep. At the moment, I was bone tired but wired. I needed a nap, and I needed a beer to help me on my way.

"I'll be in the kitchen."

"You can help me with Lora Jean first," she said disapprovingly. I wasn't sure why it took two people to escort a skinny girl to a couch, but I acquiesced.

Frieda led LJ into the living room, pushed two cats off the sofa, and ordered her to lie down. LJ responded with a scowl. "Doc didn't do much for Reilly. I'm not sure I want him to work on me."

"Lora Jean! That's an awful thing to say," said Frieda. "Doc is a very capable doctor and you know it." She sighed. "Reilly was beyond help long before Doc arrived."

"It's just a cold, LJ," I said. "How much harm can he do?"

My contribution brought a sharp look from Frieda. "I need a beer," I said, and headed to the kitchen.

Frieda followed me. She was always baking and cleaning. She went to the sink and proceeded to scrub a cookie sheet. I felt her disapproving stare found the opener and flipped off the cap. I drained about half the bottle, then turned to her and asked, "Do you think Reilly killed himself?"

"It sounds like you do," she replied without looking at me.

"I wasn't saying he did. I was merely wondering how he might have died if he didn't commit suicide."

Frieda rubbed a cookie sheet with a rough sponge. "I don't know," she said finally. "You're smart. You figure it out."

"What's that supposed to mean?" I asked.

"What it means is that I haven't thought about it one way or the other because thinking about it won't change anything. He's dead and he needs to be buried. That's all I know."

"Sarah seems to think that Reilly didn't kill himself."

Frieda turned around and scowled at me. "No one cares what Sarah says. Sarah thinks one of them killed him because they all hate him for one reason or another. But the night he died, he invited them all to the house for a meeting. None of them cared enough to show up. I don't see any of them deciding after all these years to kill him."

"So Reilly shot himself?"

Frieda pursed her lips. "If that's what he did, then damn his soul to hell for not saying good-bye."

I got up and patted Frieda on the shoulder. "I think I should go," I said.

"You'll stay here," insisted Frieda. "Just like Reilly would have wanted. I've made up the upstairs bedroom at the end of the hall."

Upstairs were eight bedrooms, including a huge master bedroom. Each of the bedrooms was bright and warm, and furnished with contemporary but comfortable furniture. Each room also seemed to come with its own sleeping cat. I found the room at the end of the hall, threw my bag on the floor, and stretched out on the bed. My eyes burned and my head throbbed, residual symptoms of the previous night's bout with insomnia. Prison makes a person sleep lightly, and I hadn't quite kicked the habit. Here in Reilly's house, I found myself sinking into the soft quilt, the thick down and the cozy room beckoning like a narcotic. I counted down from thirty, then sat up. Doc Adams was on his way over and I needed to talk to him.

I forced myself off the bed and headed downstairs. I took my beer and peanuts to the kitchen, then went to the study. The door was shut. Frieda appeared, then realized I was going into the room. "It's not been cleaned since he died," she said. When she saw I was undeterred, she scurried away.

I opened the door slowly, almost reverently. I stood for a moment in a short hallway formed by ceiling-high shelves that lined the interior walls. I could see the coffee table that fronted the couch on which Reilly died and the door at the other end of the study. A pillow was on the end of the table closest to me, probably to prop up Reilly's broken foot. Reilly's crutches were leaning against the arm of the couch.

I stepped into the room slowly, glancing toward the couch, but focusing my gaze elsewhere. I reached a free-standing bookcase and took a deep breath, then moved forward. I focused on a Christmas tree behind the couch, its lights still twinkling merrily. Finally, I turned and looked at the sofa and its dark tragic stain.

Reilly was apparently sitting on the left end of the sofa as I faced it. The bullet entered his chest, and he fell toward the middle, his blood draining onto the seat cushion. The stuffing had been torn from the left back cushion near the bottom, probably to recover the bullet that killed him.

I imagined Reilly in this room deciding whether to live or die, making an irreversible decision to squeeze the trigger and end his life. Then a second, far darker image flashed in my mind. The gun is in the hands of someone else. Reilly isn't weighing the virtues of more tomorrows. Unable to move because of his broken foot, he's waiting in terror of having his life stolen, maybe by someone he knew.

I finished my beer, then took a fresh one and the can of peanuts to the sunroom and stretched out in a reclining chair. I had just kicked off my shoes when a gray tabby jumped onto my chest. I tried to place the cat to one side, but the feline wasn't interested in moving. After a few minutes, I gave up and the cat curled up on top of me, closed its eyes, and purred loudly.

I ate half a can of nuts and finished my second beer, then drifted into a light sleep filled with dreams and voices, none of which made sense. When I opened my eyes, I was staring at Doc.

"I hear you're sick."

"Not me, Doc. LJ."

He glanced at the empty beer bottles on the floor. "Still not sleeping?"

"I take cat naps. But I'm having trouble with fur balls."

Doc chuckled. "They can be a nuisance."

I led him into the living room. He sat next to LJ and felt her pulse. "Okay, what hurts?"

"My head. I think it's going to explode."

"That would be disgusting," said Doc with a laugh followed by a cough. "Well, it's too late for an asafetida bag. In the old days, we'd prescribe skunk fat and opossum fat mixed with turpentine to be rubbed on the chest three or four times a day.

With the weather being so warm, it wouldn't be hard to find fresh road kill of both species." He sighed and handed her a tissue. "Blow," he said. LJ obliged. Doc took the tissue, opened it, and gazed at its contents. "Never could read tea leaves, but nothing like looking at snot to get a reading on what's going on inside the head. And yours is a brown-green mess. You've got a sinus infection, and for that I prescribe..."

I thought about a bag of skunk guts hanging from LJ's neck. From her expression, I surmised she was thinking the same thing.

"Keflex should do it. Expensive but effective. I'll call it in. You'll be back in action in a day or two."

Doc looked at me. "I could prescribe something to help you sleep," he said.

"Beer works and I can get it without a prescription. But there is something you can help me with."

I motioned to him with my head and led Doc into the kitchen. "So Reilly really killed himself?" I asked him, pulling the cap off a bottle.

Doc stiffened. "That was my professional opinion."

"And no autopsy was performed?"

"My opinion was enough for the sheriff. Why isn't that enough for you?"

Doc turned to leave, then said, "Make sure Lora Jean gets plenty of rest and takes the antibiotics for ten days."

I put down my beer. "Just a few more questions. Reilly supposedly shot himself in the chest." Doc gave me a pained look. "I just want to understand something. He shot himself with his right hand?" I sat down in a kitchen chair, my right side pressed against the armrest. I then touched my chest with my right index finger. "Like this?"

"Maybe. What's your point?"

"I'm thinking that if I shot myself like this, the exit wound would be up toward my left shoulder, which would put a hole toward the middle of the back of the couch. But the couch in the study has a hole in the back cushion near the bottom—by the arm."

Doc put down his bag. He seemed perplexed. "The exit wound was through his left kidney."

I turned my hand so that the tip of my index finger, my heart, and my kidney were all roughly aligned. At this angle, my wrist and elbow were bent at right angles. "Seems a bit awkward, doesn't it? Actually, it seems unlikely."

"I don't have time for this." said Doc, reaching for his bag. "If you want to think someone killed him, then think it."

"I just want to know the truth, Doc. What if someone murdered him?"

Doc rubbed his eyes. "Reilly was a complex man with lots of demons. Maybe he was going to die anyway. Do I want some old, bitter fool in this town going to prison because he got pissed off and shot Reilly?"

Doc's answer surprised me. "Doesn't it depend on which fool we're talking about and what Reilly might have done to him?"

"Are you so pure that you want to make that judgment?" asked Doc, angrily. "You go rooting around in all this old dirt and you may find the truth, but you may not know what to do with it. Take a look at me and think about sending me to jail at my age. Reilly would still be dead. No good would come of knowing that truth. Why bother?"

"The law says..."

"Poo the law. Let Reilly rest in peace. Let us all rest in peace."

"What are you hiding, Doc?"

"Go home, Shep. This doesn't concern you and you don't have any idea who you might hurt." Doc stared at me, pleading with his eyes, then took his bag and walked out as fast as his old legs would carry him.

I sat for a moment, playing with my finger gun, wondering why people were so afraid of the truth.

Chapter 10

I sat with LJ until Frieda arrived with her prescription. In the meantime, she talked about her friends and where they were going for Christmas, but not about Reilly. With Frieda again in charge, I fetched another beer, and went back to the sunroom to resume my nap. For me, sleeping in the daytime is not a recreational endeavor, but a necessity. At night, the demons visit so often I'm almost afraid of nodding off. By contrast, most of my daytime dreams are like those of any normal person.

A few minutes later, I heard the door open and sensed Frieda's presence. Naps in Lyle seemed hard to come by. I opened my eyes and looked at her. She was staring into space, the corner of her mouth twitching. Her eyes glistened and her cheeks were awash with tears. "Twenty years," she said, "and I didn't say good-bye. What am I going to do now?"

"Trust me on this, Frieda. You'll be taken care of and so will LJ."

"Thank you," she said regaining her composure, then added, "I never believed what they said about you."

I closed my eyes, briefly considering possible "whats" and "theys" that Frieda might be alluding to. But sleep pulled at me and I gave into it willingly.

I was on a beach somewhere sipping rum and cokes with

Amy Stewart when suddenly I was transported back to Lyle, and Frieda and LJ were hovering over me. "Some men were here with a coffin," said Frieda. "Laura Jean let them in while I was in the bathroom. Then I found this note on the front door. What is going on?"

The note was simple: "GET OUT OF TOWN BEFORE SOMETHING BAD HAPPENS." It was the tone that was strange. Was it a threat or a plea? The note paper was ruled and punched for a three-hole binder. All three of its holes had been torn, making it obvious that the paper had been pulled from a notebook.

"The men said they'd leave the coffin open," added Frieda. "I told them they'd made a mistake, but they said you said it was okay."

The last part of her statement managed to establish both blame and disapproval. "Jason was charging Reilly's fans to view the body," I said. "I thought it more appropriate that the viewing be here and free."

Frieda nodded. "I see now. Yes. Thank you."

I didn't tell her I had other plans for Reilly.

"He's in the living room and so are my things," said LJ. "I can't go in there."

The open casket was at the end of the room. A stray beam of sunlight danced across Reilly's waxen face. I watched as a male tabby cat appeared on the closed end of the coffin. He walked confidently toward Reilly's head, his tail raised in a question mark. When the cat was half way across the coffin, his gait slowed and his tail twitched nervously. He continued to move forward in a crouched position, until he came to the edge of the opening. The cat stepped gingerly on Reilly's chest, his head bobbing as he took in the scent of the dead body. He looked up, his mouth open—it was the feline's way of tasting what he had inhaled. A moment later, he was on the floor, scurrying away. I could see by the fluff of his tail that he had encountered something frightening. I wondered if the brave tabby would spread the news to the others that Reilly had used up his nine lives and was no longer of this earth.

Lora Jean and Frieda gathered behind. "Who is that?" whispered Lora Jean.

"That is what Reilly looked like before you were born," explained Frieda in a slightly louder whisper.

Lora Jean approached the casket, "What you see is Mr. Heartwood of the late fifties," I said. "Reilly in his prime."

"Reilly with hair," added an uncertain Lora Jean. "I never seen Reilly wear a wig before."

"Another of Jason Grubb's bright ideas," I said.

"God have mercy on us," said Frieda genuflecting.

I met Frieda's eyes and like the cat tasting what he couldn't smell, I saw what I couldn't hear. "I'm sorry," I said. "Perhaps I should close the lid."

Frieda shook her head. "Later."

I took a deep breath. "Lora Jean, could you show me where you keep the aspirin?"

Lora Jean made a face. "But you know . . ."

Her protest ended when Frieda touched Reilly's cheek. LJ turned quickly and walked out. I followed her to the kitchen. "I'm sorry," said LJ. "I didn't think about Frieda wanting to be alone with Reilly."

"You did fine," I said.

She studied a fingernail for a moment, then asked, "Are you going to sleep in this house with that dead body? I mean, jeze, I couldn't."

I swallowed two aspirin. "I've slept in places with a lot worse," I said.

"Prison must really suck," said LJ. Whether she was referring to me or to her father, or both of us, I wasn't sure. I put my glass in the dishwasher, then asked, "Did Reilly ever mention the name Hollinger and why he adopted it as his stage name?"

"God, no," replied Lora Jean, rolling her eyes.

"I gather I've asked a dumb question?"

"The most. I asked Reilly about it once. Chewed my butt out but good."

"Reilly had a temper?"

"Not usually," she said.

I could see that the interaction still bothered her, but I persisted. "Do you know why he got so heated?"

"No, and neither did Frieda. He apologized—sort of—but that's the only time it came up when I was around." Lora Jean bit her lower lip. "It feels strange to be pissed at someone who's dead."

I put my hand under Lora Jean's chin and lifted her head so that she faced me. "No matter how someone dies, people are always left behind. The dead have what comes next. The living have all the unfinished stuff, like arguments that weren't settled, things that were never done, words that were never said. When someone kills himself, you can't help but feel cheated, like he should have said good-bye, or you should have said something.

There's no right or wrong about it. Just feel what you feel, and let it play itself out." I had just synthesized a few thousand dollars' worth of therapy into a couple of sentences. I patted her on the cheek and she smiled back at me.

"Thanks," she said. "I didn't believe he was dead until I saw him in the coffin." Her eyes welled up, but she didn't cry. "I know he liked me. I hope he knew I liked him." A single tear rolled down her cheek, then dripped onto the floor. "I just didn't tell him."

"He liked you very much," I said, wiping her cheek with my finger.

I handed her a table napkin and she blew her nose.

"Thanks," she said, then asked hesitantly, "Did someone shoot Mr. Heartwood? I heard you and Doc arguing."

"I don't know," I replied.

"But you're going to find out? Right? I mean, even if one of Doc's old friends shot Mr. Heartwood, it doesn't seem right that he should get away with murder."

"No. It wouldn't be right."

"So you're going to find out who did it?"

I was beginning to appreciate how much Reilly had meant to LJ. My first reaction was envy. I hadn't felt that close to anyone in a long time. "I'll do what I can. But you have to remember, I'm not a professional investigator."

"It's not fair," she said, her eyes now flooding with tears. She buried her head against my shoulder and sobbed while I stroked her hair.

A few minutes later, her emotions spent, Lora Jean went upstairs to take a nap. I found Frieda in the kitchen looking at recipes. "All these people are coming, and I don't know how I'm going to feed them."

"You're not expected to feed them," I said, but Frieda continued flipping through a stack of file cards. "You said that Reilly invited everyone over the night he died. Who exactly did he invite and who showed up?"

Frieda shrugged. "Doc, Robbie, Chester Atkins, Terry, and Billy. Maybe some other folks. I don't think he actually invited Darrel Potter, but he may have. I don't think anyone came except Doc, and by that time, it was too late. Is it important?"

"I don't know," I said. "I guess I'd like to talk to them."

"You can go to the bowling alley tonight. Darrel doesn't bowl anymore, but Billy will be there and Chester still manages to bowl despite his tremors. Doc and Sarah will probably be there, too, but Doc won't be bowling."

I thought for a moment. "Where did Reilly keep his papers?"

"I don't know anything about papers. He liked to type on his computer. It's in the study—where he died."

I walked into the study. Frieda followed, but stopped at the doorway, not ready to enter the room. I looked through the drawers of Reilly's desk and found the usual collection of canceled checks, bills, and magazines. I also found a large box of condoms.

Frieda appeared, her gaze focused on me to avoid taking in the bloodstained couch. "Reilly would hand them out at school dances and football games along with a pamphlet on diseases. The sheriff made him stop, but kids asked for them anyway." She shrugged. "In this town, you buy a rubber from the druggist and he calls your mama."

Next to the desk I found a large box with a note from Robbie taped to its lid—a note indicating that the box contained the contents of Reilly's safe deposit box and a bundle of recent mail. I found the deed to the house, the insurance policies, and a file of newspaper clippings. I scanned the articles and pictures, finally finding an article about Reilly's leaving Lyle and the scandal he left behind.

The article carried the headline, "Up and Coming Singer Leaves Hometown Holding Bag" and painted a portrait of a man who abandoned those who supported him just as he was poised to achieve stardom. The gist of the story was that Reilly never had any intentions of supporting a recording studio in Lyle and had made money by selling the investors land at inflated prices. According to the writer, the Commonwealth's Attorney was looking into whether laws were broken.

I tossed the article back into the stack of clippings and it collapsed into the muck of papers, policies, mail, and old bills. I wasn't sure what I was looking for, and I didn't find it. Reilly's mail looked ordinary to me. Nothing official or compelling, no document or even a bill or paper with an unusual address. Of course, Robbie and Amy had already gone through everything. I had no way to know if anything was missing.

Then I turned the computer on. It went through its series of systems checks with blinding speed. A logo appeared, followed by a log-on prompt. "PLEASE ENTER PASSWORD." I eyed the computer's request with surprise. I tried a few of the obvious code words—Reilly's name, the name of the town, the names of the people in his town—but the computer rejected them all. I comforted myself with the realization that if I couldn't get to the files, neither could Robbie, Amy, or, for that matter, Tom. "You don't have any idea how to enter the system, do you?" I asked Frieda.

"I don't know what the system is," she said defensively.

I asked her the names of Reilly's cats, but none of the names was the needed password. After ten minutes, Frieda said, "I don't have time to be playing with a computer. I've got meals to fix and a sick child to tend to." She left the room, leaving me one word away from Reilly's private files. I started over, playing with variations of people's names, Reilly's songs, anything I could think of that Reilly might have chosen to secure his computer and easily remember.

"Why does everything have to be so damn difficult?" I asked, glaring at the blinking cursor. As I reached for the power switch, I answered my own question. "Because you're in Lyle."

Chapter 11

*A*fter two helpings of meatloaf, it was hard convincing Frieda I wasn't hungry for dessert. She had cooked enough for a small army and expected someone (translation, me) to eat it. I told Frieda I'd clean up. As she left the house, she said, "Lora Jean and I will be back in the morning. We've got lots of work to do if we're going to have a proper viewing." The reason for the statement was unclear, but I suspected I was being told not to sleep late.

I was clearing the table when I heard the front door open and a disembodied voice call out, "Hello?"

I found Amy in the foyer. "Hi," I said, almost adding, "I was dreaming about you."

"I hope I'm not intruding." She looked at me through clear eyes.

"Not at all. I was just cleaning up."

She followed me to the kitchen. "You must think I'm crazy," she said, then laughed. "Actually, I am. I suffer from depression and anxiety. I've had to deal with it as long as I can remember. Sometimes my medication and I don't get along."

I put my plate into the dishwasher. "I didn't think anything of the kind," I said trying to sound convincing.

"I'm sure you did, but you're far too considerate to say so. I had a nervous breakdown a few years ago. It wasn't the first time, but it was the worst. I still have little episodes and it takes me a while to turn all the lights back on." A black tomcat jumped up on the table, walked over, and butted her chin with his head. "Oh, my," said Amy.

"He was just saying howdy. In cat language, it means, 'I like you.' "

She scratched the cat under his chin. "Tom won't let me have a cat." The cat nudged her again and she smiled with delight. "I didn't understand what was happening to me at the time," she said, apparently referring again to her breakdown. "Tom was working on a redevelopment project that involved block busting. People who were old and frail were badgered until they left. I saw their faces on the news and it made me sick. Then the calls started. The phone would ring at all hours of the night. Tom would be out somewhere. One night, I just went off. After I got out of the hospital, Tom promised he wouldn't do a deal like that again. He built a house here, but he rarely stays in it. He's got an apartment in D.C."

"Sounds like he can be pretty ruthless," I said.

"If you're asking if Tom is capable of murder, I'd say no. But, in a fit of rage, he could hurt someone." She rolled up her sleeve. "He burned me here with a fireplace poker," she said. "We were fighting about something while he was stirring the logs in the fireplace. He just turned and touched the poker to my arm. He said it was an accident. But it wasn't. That's why I was asking the questions after the council meeting. I was afraid you might know something that implicated Tom." Amy pursed her lips to stifle a rush of emotion. "Tom's not the person I married.

I may be divorcing him, but I don't want him getting into real trouble."

"Is that what you were discussing at lunch? A settlement?"

The question took Amy by surprise. "You don't miss much," she said. "Tom's pleading poverty. He's broke, he says, but that's not my fault. He had a lot riding on developing the old music studio property. When Reilly declined to sell the poor farm, Tom lost a bundle. But as I said, I can't be concerned with that. He has to come to terms with the situation and get on with his life and let me get on with mine."

"And what would it mean to Tom—and you—if Reilly had agreed to sell the farm?"

Amy smiled wickedly. "Tom would have made decent money and paid most of it to me." She touched her upper lip with her tongue. "So what are you going to do with the poor farm?"

I tried to read her eyes to determine the answer she wanted. "I haven't decided. I've considered booting the old folks out and building a ranch where rich city folk could come and shoot wild animals released from cages. Maybe I could tether the rich folk to stakes and let the animals take a good whack at them. The possibilities are endless."

Amy laughed. "I think you need medication."

"Maybe I can sell the farm to you and you can use it to torture Tom."

Amy shook her head. "I don't think that way."

"Sorry. I said I would defer to Reilly's wishes. That may not make Tom or his clients happy."

"Reilly stood up to Tom to protect the people who live on

the poor farm. The farm is the only home they know. As I see it, it's admirable that Reilly wouldn't sell the land out from under them."

"How does Tom feel about your empathy toward the poor and unwanted?"

Amy smiled at me. "I don't really care much about what Tom thinks," she said. "But I'm glad you don't think of me as a basket case."

She flashed a smile at me, then looked into my eyes. I may have been out of circulation for a while, but the look was an invitation.

"I better be going," she said. "If you need someone to talk to while you're in Lyle, please call me."

I politely walked her to the door, and watched as she drove away.

I was certain Amy had an agenda. I just wasn't certain what it was.

Chapter 12

The Lyle Bowlarama was located on the western edge of town, one block south of Main Street. Tonight, league night, its parking lot was full. Pick-ups and four-wheel drives mingled indiscriminately with expensive imported cars, complete with leather seats and cellular telephone antennas protruding from back windows. I parked on the street and walked inside.

I was inundated by sounds—balls crashing into pins, balls hitting balls, pinsetters clanking, people cheering. My nose was treated to the smell of stale beer, cigarette smoke, hot fat, vinegar, and ketchup. I entered at lane twenty and strolled past the settees, threading my way through a forest of people who seemed to be in motion without going anywhere. The league players were hanging around waiting for the lanes to clear of other patrons and for league play to start.

Sarah was sitting at a table with Doc. Chester Atkins was sitting alone at the adjacent table drinking water. His eyes locked on me like lasers, following me to Sarah's table and then to my chair.

"Now, what business do you have coming here?" asked Chester.

"Behave yourself Chester," said Sarah. "Maybe Shep will sell you the poor farm." She drained a glass of beer, belched, then patted my hand.

Doc looked at me. "I'm sorry if I sounded insensitive this afternoon. Reilly was a good man and a good friend. I know you think you're doing the right thing by asking questions and such, but you've got to let it go. Nothing you do will bring him back, and dredging through the past is only going to open old wounds."

Chester stood up and came over to me. "You don't want to sell the farm? Fine. But you don't have to come here and bother folks when they're trying to have a little fun. It's a crime, that's what it is."

"So is murder," said Sarah.

Chester waved at her in disgust and walked away.

"Chester didn't kill him," said Doc, "if that's what you were thinking."

"I wasn't thinking it," I said, "but I am curious about the meeting Reilly called the night he died."

Doc said, "He called a meeting because he wanted to convey some good news."

"Did Reilly ever mention to you what his good news was?"

"Don't do this," pleaded Doc. "You're just going to dredge up a lot of history that would best be buried with Reilly."

"If Reilly ever gets buried," countered Sarah. "People in this town are such cowards."

Doc glanced at both of us. "I heard that Rose wants Shep to apologize for something Mary did in exchange for Reilly getting a funeral. Reilly could be buried tomorrow."

Sarah, her eyes fixed on Doc, said, "Whatever Mary did to Rose she had coming."

"You're hopeless," said Doc. He looked at me. "You see what's happening?"

I ignored him. "What's with Billy?" I asked. "I mean, why doesn't he just ignore Rose?"

"Because Rose has got him by his heavenly balls," snapped Sarah, "ifen he's got any."

"For Christ's sake," pleaded Doc. "What's the point of this? Mary's dead. What is it going to matter to her? Rose is alive— sort of. It might make her life better if Shep said he was sorry. It would also get Reilly buried and all this speculation about how he died will be forgotten. We need to move on."

Sarah shook her head. "No way."

"Is someone going to tell me what Mom did?"

"I don't want to talk about it," said Doc, who promptly got up and walked away.

"I heard pieces of the story, but Terry was there. He's down on lane sixteen." Sarah stood up. "I need to warm up. We can talk later."

I found Terry wiping down his ball with alcohol. "Hey, Shep. Lanes are pretty oily tonight. I need a dry ball to get my hook working."

"Sarah says you know what Rose wants me to apologize for."

Terry put his ball in the return tray, then brought his hands to his lips, as if praying. He nodded a few times but didn't say anything. He was priming himself to tell a story. Terry took story-telling very seriously.

"Your mother was a proud woman," he said softly. "She was also stubborn, at least about certain things. But most of all she had a sense of what was fair and she was never shy about making sure people got what they deserved—good or bad.

"The Daughters of the Shenandoah Valley used to sponsor Valley Days. Maybe you remember them. They celebrated the history of the region. Anyway, it was a big deal to some of the folks around here. To be chosen to deliver a speech and to wear a period costume at Valley Days was a big honor. 'Course, the Daughters were particular about who got into the society and more particular who they let onto the Valley Days' Committee.

"Mary had all the ancestral requirements, but the Committee concluded that she wasn't high enough on the social ladder to get in. For years, Lyle's representative had been an Abernathy—either Rose's mother or her aunt. Rose was a member, but the society wasn't happy about her drinking. So, when it came time for a Lyle member of the society to chair the Valley Days committee, the Daughters had a problem. Rose was the obvious choice but couldn't be counted on to be sober.

"The Daughters found the solution in your mother. Being forgiving, open-minded folks, they decided that your mother's social status had improved. After all, she had been to college and married a career diplomat. She had contacts in Washington and might be able to enlist a Congressman or Senator to give a speech. The Daughters inducted your mother and named her as chairman, or chairperson, or chair—whatever you're supposed to say these days—of the celebration committee. It was your mother's idea to ask anyone who wanted to represent an ancestor to write in with his or her idea. She assembled some of the locals, lots of them no more than a month's pay away from the poor farm, and selected the best ideas. Rose wasn't made part of the committee and her ideas weren't accepted."

I felt a sense of relief. If Rose was still moping because she'd been left out of Valley Days twenty years before, it didn't seem too humbling to suggest that maybe my mother could have handled it better. "Doesn't sound like such a big deal to me," I said.

"Your mom," continued Terry, "held a party at Reilly's house. I mean Rose's old house. Rose wasn't invited, but she showed up anyway demanding to be seated at the head of the table. Mary told her that she could join the other guests, but Rose was belligerent. I'll never forget your mother's words: 'You gave up your claim to the head of this table years ago. You treated my mother and me like slaves. I'll be damned if I'll take orders from you now. So sit anywhere else or get out.' Rose went off and started screaming. Few heard what Mary had said, but Rose made enough noise that her humiliation was complete. As the story evolved, your mother called her a drunken bitch and threw a drink in her face, but I heard what she said. To add insult to injury, after this episode, Rose was thrown out of the Daughters altogether."

"What did Mom mean about being treated like slaves?"

Terry looked at his feet. "Maybe you should hear this from someone else."

I gave him an insistent look and he groaned. "Your grandmother cleaned house for the Abernathy's." Terry swallowed and shook his head. "And so did your mother. Rose watched them as they scrubbed, gave them orders, and complained that they were lazy. Your mother took the abuse and the money and went to college. I can't say your mother handled the Valley Days situation with good Christian kindness, but it's hard to fault her for taking her shot when she had it. Rose wants you to apologize because she wants revenge. She wants to humiliate Mary and you."

I nodded. "And people say the spirit of Christmas has been forgotten."

"What are you going to do?"

"I'm thinking about getting a shovel and burying Reilly myself."

I bought a soda, then scanned the alley for Chester. I made eye contact with a man standing nearby, then realized it was Councilman Drexel Seymour. He was wearing a suit, his tie stuck between the buttons of his shirt. "I love and hate this game," said Drexel with the rhythm of a well-used line.

"It'll get to you," I said.

"It really is wonderful," he continued. "It's not like tennis. Don't get me wrong. I love tennis. It's just tennis players I can't stand."

I heard the loneliness in the man's voice and tried to act sympathetic. "They can be vicious."

"Really. Here, it's just you against the pins." He sighed, making it clear the pins were winning. "It's really fascinating when you think about it. I mean, the game brings together people from all walks of life and imbues them with a common goal. Movers and shakers shoulder-to-shoulder with rednecks, hayseeds, and bumpkins."

"Amazing how they stand it as long as they do," I said, my sympathy exhausted.

"Gee," said the Councilman, "I believe it's my turn. See you."

I found Reverend Billy standing on the approach at lane nine. The ball seemed tiny against his enormous girth as he waddled toward the line. He let the ball go and it hung desperately on the edge of the gutter. Just when it seemed it might break to the inside of the alley, it dropped away and was swallowed by the machinery. He rolled again, but turned away before the ball was halfway down the lane. Nor did Billy turn when the ball crashed into the pins, wiping out all but two. He grabbed a towel and left the settee without waiting for commentary from his teammates. He walked toward me without seeing me. I thought he would pass me altogether when he suddenly noticed me. "I thought you left," he said.

"Not yet."

"I guess you want to ask me about Rose and the apology."

I hadn't remembered seeing Billy so nervous. "Something like that."

Billy's stomach rose and fell as he tried to catch his breath. A bead of sweat trickled down his cheek and he mopped his face with a towel. "I'll call you. Tomorrow."

"No you won't, Billy." I took a deep breath. "One of us is going to do something he doesn't want to do. Either you bury Reilly and take Rose's best shot, or I give my mother's worst enemy a victory she couldn't have won when my mother was alive. Reilly deserves a funeral and my mother deserves her dignity."

I waded through the crowd toward lane one. I spotted Chester sitting alone staring into space. His brow was furrowed and his lips moved slightly, as if he were conversing with someone. I was reluctant to interrupt. I had seen the same brooding look on my mother's face when she was lost in her past. Sometimes it was a letter that sent her back. Sometimes it was word that another childhood name had gone to dust. The moments were private, moments when time rolled backwards and events were relived, or a voice was heard as distinctly as when it came from living flesh. And there were moments when some malfeasance was revisited and corrected, if only in her mind. I approached Chester cautiously, hoping to catch his attention without startling him.

I reached the table and was looking for a sign of recognition when Chester spoke: "Just because I'm not looking at you doesn't mean I don't know you're there."

"You need to accept the fact that I'm going to be around until I get some answers," I said. "The sooner I get 'em, the sooner I'll be out of your hair."

I was sounding like a local.

Chester snorted a laugh. "I believe you." I came a few steps closer and reached for a chair. "Just 'cause I haven't gotten up and walked away don't mean I've invited you to stay. I told you, I don't have anything to say to you. I don't care much for people who go snooping in other folks' business."

"I'm not snooping."

"Well, it seems like it to me, so what's the difference?"

"The difference," I said angrily, "is that Reilly made it my business when he gave me the poor farm. Like it or not, the decision to sell the farm is mine. Until I decide one way or the other, it's in your best interest to answer my questions and make me feel happy."

Chester regarded me coldly, then looked away. After a few

moments, he closed his eyes. "Reilly ruined me. If I hadn't gotten a job at this bowling alley, I'd be living at the poor farm for sure. So Reilly leaves me a message on my answering machine saying he has something to tell me, some news. He tells me to come by Rose's house, I mean his house. I call him and tell him I'm not coming, that I don't care to hear news, good or bad. He can't get it through his head. Maybe the stroke made him nuts or something, but he starts to talk like we're best friends. I hang up. Rose calls me, so I know he invited her, too. I don't know who else. Rose said she'd done about the same thing as I did."

"But you went anyway." I was guessing.

He stared at me a long time before nodding. "Robbie called and said Reilly was pretty broke up when no one showed. I parked in town and walked up to the house. I looked in the window. I couldn't see Reilly, but I could hear voices. I wasn't going in to get hollered at, so I left." Chester looked at me. "I heard what sounded like a single shot. I came back here to get a beer, then called the sheriff."

"Sheriff Belamy said that Doc called him."

"The deputy told me the sheriff was already on his way, but he didn't say why. I guess Doc had showed up for the meeting and found Reilly."

"Did the sheriff ever ask you any questions?"

Chester laughed. "You think someone shot Reilly. I guess I got what you might call a motive. But I didn't shoot him and the sheriff knows it. Anyway, Doc ruled it a suicide."

"You heard something like a gunshot, but you didn't go inside the house?"

"Why would I? I didn't want to know if one of my friends

shot him." He stood up. "I need to warm up."

I watched Chester hit the head pin, leaving the impossible seven and ten pin split. Chester rolled a gutter ball trying to slide the ten into the six. On his next frame on the other lane, he left the five pin, then missed his spare attempt by the width of the ball. He came back to the table, but didn't sit down.

"Why do you think Reilly quit singing?"

Chester lit a cigarette. "People say it was Rose," he said nervously. "I doubt it. Rose likes to pretend that she's important enough to ruin a man's career, but Reilly loved singing too much. There are a lot of other stories, but I can't say I really know."

Chester's voice suggested he might know more than he was saying. Or maybe it was just me hearing things. "And who is C.C. Hollinger?"

Chester blew a cloud of smoke. "I don't know, but I heard about a colored man named Hollinger who died in jail in Tyler City. I got no idea why Reilly would use his name."

I started to ask another question when Chester stood up again. "I think I've had enough questions and you don't seem to be running out of them. My advice to you is to quit thinking about his old enemies. If anyone from Reilly's past had enough guts to kill him, they'd have done it a long time ago. If someone shot him, you need to look at recent history, not at what's been done for years." He turned and shuffled away, his tired walk making him look older than his years.

I walked through the crowd, catching snippets of conversation about ten pins, oil, and making babies. The high rollers exchanged high fives. The losers cursed and gritted their teeth.

I stepped outside. The cool air felt good on my face. As I approached my car, I saw someone standing by the driver's side door. The person turned, but in the dim light I caught a glimpse of a tall, youngish male before he disappeared into the shadows. I found a sheet of white paper pinned against my windshield by the wiper blade. I pulled the paper free, then unlocked the car door and turned on the headlights. Like the note Frieda and Laura Jean had found earlier, this paper was torn from a three-ring binder. The note read: "YOU'RE NOT LISTENING. LEAVE NOW!"

When I arrived back at the house, I realized just how tired I really was. I went to the kitchen and opened a beer, then headed to the living room.

Moonlight streamed into the room from large windows, muting the room's colors. Reilly's coffin was a bright silver monolith in the semi-darkness. A chair was close by and I imagined Frieda sitting with Reilly, trying to deal with issues that his untimely death had left open.

I sat in the chair and tried to think reverent thoughts. None came to mind. I wasn't ready to deal with the reality of his death. I was stuck on the how and why.

"So here we are," I said finally. "And I don't know if you killed yourself or not. You know and I know that no one in Lyle is ever going to say anything that might implicate anyone else in your death. So if you want me to find out who killed you, I need your help. And I need you to tell me what to do."

To my relief, nothing happened. No voices, no apparitions, no icon dripping blood. Only silence. What I was going to do was my decision, and I had already made it.

I stood up and touched Reilly's cheek. "I'm going to make a phone call to some friends of mine who can talk to the dead. I hope you don't mind."

I went to the kitchen and retrieved the cordless phone, then tapped out the number of Gus Jaynes.

Gus once worked for the FBI. I met him several years ago during the investigation that led to my indictment. Gus was trying to put me in jail, and I was fighting like hell to stop him. Gus made no bones about how he felt. I was a scumbag and belonged in prison. But Gus was of the old school, meaning the truth still mattered to him. Lucky for me.

When I was beaten and stabbed by a drug dealer in prison, some of the people who had testified against me—the folks who had forgotten the truth for one reason or another—began to have moments of conscience. Someone contacted Gus and the truth came out in dribs and drabs. Gus pursued the evidence that would exonerate me, but the legal system is hard to put in reverse. New trials are hard to come by under normal circumstances. With prosecutors and government agencies involved in a conspiracy to obstruct justice, the system reacted to protect its own.

Gus came to visit me more in my last year than anyone else. He now believed in my innocence, and his role in my wrongful conviction haunted him. I remember consoling him, telling him that my predicament was not his fault, but his faith in the justice system had been seriously shaken. Eventually, I was granted a new trial and exonerated. The FBI rewarded Gus by firing him.

After I was released, and after he was fired, he sued the FBI and the case was settled. Now he's an investigator for defense lawyers. He still tells it like he sees it, but looks with his eyes open a little wider than before.

Because of the hour, my call must have frightened him. "Gus, I'm fine," I said several times. "I can't sleep, that's all. But I need your help."

We talked for thirty minutes or so. I gave him a list of names of people who knew Reilly—including Tom Stewart. Gus promised that he and a forensics specialist name Zak Tully would be in Lyle in the morning.

I went to bed knowing that tomorrow Reilly would be asked to testify in his own behalf. I hoped he would forgive me.

Chapter 13

*A*round 2:00 in the morning, I woke the first time in a cold sweat. My heart was racing because my brain wasn't sure where I was. I sat up, disturbing the half dozen cats snoozing soundly on the bed with me. In the darkness, I saw a pair of green eyes staring at me, conveying annoyance at my failure to understand bedtime protocol. I apologized, then leaned back against the headboard.

My first few weeks in prison had established this pattern. The minimum-security prison I was assigned to was an open facility. No bars to lock you in. No bars to protect you. The enemy of sleep is fear, and uncertainty is the father of fear. I entered the facility afraid for my physical person, but quickly realized my head to be in greatest peril.

Most minimum-security prisoners are not the male rapists depicted in the movies. They are ordinary men with ordinary needs. When the lights go out, the first thing that struck me was the sobbing. Grown men cry themselves to sleep or at least try to. Some even wet the bed. With a sentence of twelve years, I was fearful of what prison would do to me. I guess I was afraid of humiliating myself. I craved privacy, a moment when I could cry or scream into my pillow and no one, not even a guard, would see or hear me. As close as I got were the hours after most of the others had fallen asleep. That's when I would wake up. It's when I wake up even now.

I shed a few tears the first couple of weeks in prison, but mostly I thought about Anna and the life we'd planned. We were made for each other, two young adults with good jobs enjoying what the world had to offer those with disposable income. She loved me until just before the end of my trial. That's when she gave up on me.

I thought she held up well even as the testimony against me piled up. I could have copped a plea, but I wasn't going to admit to a lie. Anna struggled hard to believe I was innocent. But the lies told against me were just too convincing to leave room for any reasonable doubt. She reached the same conclusion as the jury, and hated me for it. In her mind, I was guilty of being a clever, unethical lawyer, who had to be punished. I saw the anger in her eyes when they took me away, and see it still in my dreams.

I sat up and squeezed a pillow against my chest. For a moment, I thought I could smell her hair, and I had to endure the pain of that memory. I hadn't heard from her since being absolved of my so-called crimes against society. I suspect my conviction for killing our marriage still stood.

Then I heard something outside my door. I listened, thinking it might be a cat, but then I heard it again. "Shep?"

I flipped on a light and found Amy standing in the doorway. She was wearing an overcoat and carrying a small overnight bag. I pulled back the covers and watched as her coat slid to the floor. My brain screamed a futile warning, but I was long past the point of no return. "I thought you might need some company," she said, lying down next to me, "and I know I do."

Then I saw the box of condoms that she'd placed on the nightstand. "I saw where Reilly kept them when I was doing the audit," she said, then giggled mischievously. "I hope there's enough."

You've got to appreciate a woman with that kind of optimism.

I woke before sunrise with a pounding headache. I was alone. The cats had all run in either fear or disgust. Amy had showered and left a few hours earlier. I was glad she came and relieved she left. She was physically exhausting, and her mood shifts—even in that short time—were taxing. She had arrived giddy and playful. She left withdrawn and shaking. I heard her looking through her bag, cursing. She had apparently packed the wrong medication. She recovered enough to give me a peck on the cheek as she left, but I had misgivings about the whole interlude. It's one thing to be messing with a guy's wife. It's another to be viewed as taking advantage of a sick woman. I'm sure my shrink would have something to say about my tumble with Amy and about how I felt when it was over. But the bottom line is that both Amy and I needed a good lay and we used each other to get it.

We hadn't talked much. Amy had asked me again if I believed Reilly was murdered. I said I did. Then she'd asked if I was going to find out who did it. When I said probably not, she'd said, "You think Tom did it." The remark struck me as odd, not only because I hadn't suggested that he had, but because the remark was not followed by a spousal denial. Before more could be said on the subject, she was in the shower.

I took a shower and dressed, then lay down again. I was

awakened a second time by a knock on the door. Frieda appeared, a scowl on her face. I immediately worried that I hadn't covered-up my roll in the sheets with Amy. But then Frieda said, "There are men downstairs. They said they had an appointment with you, but they look like cops to me. You aren't in trouble, are you?"

"No. It's okay," I said getting up. "I called them." She wasn't convinced. "Frieda, they're here to determine whether Reilly killed himself."

"How do they do that?"

"They examine the scene and they examine the body."

I could see the rage burning in Frieda's eyes. "Have you no respect for the dead?!"

"I do. And I think Reilly deserves to have the question about how he died laid to rest."

"I don't want you to do this. You don't have the right."

I rubbed my eyes, then let my headache take over my sense of reason. "Everybody in this God damned town has an opinion about what I should do and how I should do it. So I'm going to do what I think is right in the only way I know how."

Tears welled up in her eyes. "Your breakfast is in the kitchen," she said. "I'll be at home if you need me."

I came to my senses, but not soon enough. I took her arm. "Listen to me. The sheriff didn't do his job. Doc is lying to me. Everyone I talk to is hiding something. I don't have any choice."

She pulled from my grasp. "You have a choice and you've made it. You don't need me to make you feel better about it."

She ran down the stairs. By the time I'd finished dressing, I heard her car pulling out of the driveway. I called for Lora Jean, but there was no answer. The two of them were gone and it was probably for the best.

Coming down the stairs, I caught a whiff of sausage and bacon. Gus was in the kitchen sipping a cup of coffee. Another man—this one tall and wiry—was loading up on eggs, breakfast rolls, and meat. Gus saw me and shook his head. "Jesus, you look like hell."

"And it's good seeing you," I said. I glanced at the other guy, but he didn't acknowledge me.

"The man with the elephant appetite is Zak Tully."

Zak put down his fork and shook my hand. "Good to meet you," he said exuberantly. I wasn't sure if his enthusiasm was his nature or because of the food. How a man could stuff himself before examining a dead body was beyond me.

"We'd have been here earlier," said Gus, "but the traffic is awful all the way to Gainesville. Something about a man named C.C. Hollinger."

"That would be Reilly Heartwood," I said. "His fans knew him as C.C. Hollinger."

"One-time country singer with a couple of cross-over hits," said Zak. "Really smooth voice. Songs a tad sad, but good. You got any more biscuits?"

"Zak is a cliché come to life," said Gus. "Skinny and eats like a horse. Got a smile that makes my palms sweat. And likes dead things. I don't work with him at night because his voice gives me the creeps. But he's really good at what he does."

Zak smiled, and I immediately understood Gus's perspective.

"The body's been to the mortician?" Zak spoke in a halting

rhythm, as if he were out of breath.

"Afraid so," I answered, getting a cup of coffee. "Is that a problem?"

"Powder traces would have been removed," he said without turning away from his plate.

"What I want to know is whether it's more likely that he shot himself or more likely that someone shot him," I said. "Anything else you can tell me is icing on the cake."

Zak rolled three strips of bacon in a pancake and ate it in two bites, then washed it down with a gulp of coffee. "My examination is going to be based largely on the entry angle and trajectory of the round that killed him. Assuming the bullet went straight through the body with minimal deflection, I can make a reasonably accurate determination of the position the murder weapon was in when it was fired. Then it's a matter of probabilities regarding how the fatal wound was inflicted."

"That's what I need," I said.

Zak patted his mouth with a napkin. "Let's get to work."

From Zak's van, Zak and Gus removed a folded-up examining table and a bag of tools. We lifted what was once Reilly Heartwood from his coffin, set him on the table, and removed his shirt. I watched with an uneasy feeling, a mixture of doubt as to the propriety of disturbing the dead and fear of what Zak was going to do with Reilly's remains.

Zak was careful with the body, almost reverent. "Easy, Mr. Heartwood," he said softly as he rolled Reilly on his stomach. "This will all be over soon." His words were aimed at Reilly, but I took some comfort in them myself. At Zak's direction, Gus helped guide the table into the study while I steadied Reilly's body. Reilly had returned to the room in which he died.

Zak stood at Reilly's head and looked at me. "I'm going to explain things as I go along. If you already know the subject matter, speak up and I'll spare you the lecture. Ready?"

I wasn't sure, but I nodded anyway.

"Reilly was embalmed," said Zak. "The embalming fluid reduces the effects of rigor mortis and adds color to the skin. But the reason for embalming is still debated. In ancient times, it was probably done for religious reasons. In modern practice, it's justified as a public health measure—intended to preserve and disinfect the body before it's viewed publicly. With major internal wounds like these, the effectiveness of intravenous embalming is questionable, so I'd advise you to put this man in the ground sooner rather than later."

We positioned the table next to the sofa where Reilly had died. Zak rubbed his fingers over Reilly's back. "Here's the exit wound. It's been sutured closed." Zak looked at me. "I think it's the money. That's why we embalm people. We embalm a body before we cremate it. That's got to be a rip off." He retrieved a scalpel from a tool bag. My stomach tightened as he proceeded to open the wound. "Let's roll him over."

He found the entry wound just below the left nipple and cut the sutures away. "Now we pretend to be the bullet."

He took a metal rod from his bag and pushed it into the hole in Reilly's chest. I stepped back a few feet and watched the process from the corner of my eyes. "If the bullet hit bone and went off at an angle, we won't have a straight tunnel and I won't be able to find the exit wound," said Zak. "If I force the rod too much, I may create a tunnel and come to the wrong conclusion.

It's a matter of touch."

Minutes passed. I studied the room, the carpet, the scenery outside—anything but Zak. Then the rod tapped the examination table. Zak rolled Reilly on his side and forced it through.

I glanced at Reilly. From my vantage point, he'd been shot by a silver arrow without feathers.

Gus and Zak rolled the table closer to the sofa where Reilly had been sitting when he was shot. Carefully, the two men positioned the body as it had been found. It took some effort to get the body to bend into a sitting position. I reminded Zak of Reilly's broken foot and he extended Reilly's leg so that it rested on the coffee table. Zak placed the rod through the hole in the sofa and they stepped back.

"Interesting," said Zak, removing a camera from his bag.

My stomach thought it was anything but interesting. I swallowed hard. When Reilly's mouth opened, I'd had more forensics than I could stand. I bolted from the room, barely making it to the bathroom in time, then pressed my face to the cold floor.

"You shouldn't have been in the room," said Gus. He handed me a wet towel. "Cops do the same thing when they know the victim."

I sat up, then made it to my feet. "What's Zak doing anyway?"

"He's making measurements, looking at angles. He's serious about pretending to be the bullet. It's better not to watch."

The tornado in my stomach dissipated, and I led Gus to the sunroom. We joined half a dozen cats who were enjoying the humid air. "This is quite a house," said Gus inspecting a broadleafed plant.

I made an attempt to smile. "If it weren't in Lyle, you might even want to live here."

"So tell me, what is it you're up to?" he gently asked. Before I could answer, he jumped in, "I know you're trying to determine if Reilly was murdered. I want to know what it is you're really trying to accomplish."

I shrugged. "I just want to know how Reilly died. If he was murdered, I want to know who killed him."

"Do you? What if it was a friend of yours? What if it was someone Reilly cared about?"

"I've heard this lecture. I know what I'm doing."

"Then hear it again. Before you go down this road, you need to know what you're going to do with the truth. When I was an agent, it wasn't my decision. But I'm not an agent any more and you never were. You learn the truth and you take the fate of someone in your hands. You have no duty to tell or not tell. That's a hell of a burden. I just want you to consider what you're volunteering for."

We sat in silence for a moment. Gus inspected another plant while I rubbed my temples. "I don't know. I need to do this. I think I owe it to him."

"As long as you've weighed the consequences of pursuing the answer, I'll keep helping you." Gus rolled a leaf over and studied it carefully. "White flies," he said grimly. "Zak can get you some parasitic wasps that'll take care of them, but you better hurry. Once the flies get started, they're hard to control."

Zak popped into the room. "I need some help putting Reilly back where he was." He stared at Gus, then added, "I've packed the van."

Gus stood up. "What Zak is trying to say is that he's still

hungry, and I've got to feed him. Shep, you stay here and I'll help with Reilly.

"I'll take the data back to my office," said Zak. "I should know something tomorrow or the next day."

I thanked them both again. I saw the concern in Gus's eyes and it both frightened and comforted me. But I had set things in motion and wasn't going to turn back.

I went to the kitchen and ate what little Zak had left behind. I felt the urge to take a nap, but I had too much to do.

I called Frieda and left a message for her with her sister that Reilly was resting comfortably. I also asked her sister to remind Frieda of tomorrow's viewing. I called Robbie, got the number and address of Jeb Garrett, Reilly's attorney in Front Royal, then called Jeb and set up a meeting for later that morning. If anyone would know how Reilly planned in life to deal with the poor farm, it would be Jeb.

I had an hour or so before I had to be in Front Royal so I decided to head into town. As I was about to leave, the phone rang. It was Amy.

"Hi," she said in a friendly tone. "I'm feeling human again. Would you like to get a cup of coffee?"

"That's a nice offer," I said, "but I've got business in Front Royal. How about a raincheck?"

I heard a long pause. "I don't mean to be a pain," she said, "but I'd really like some company. Tom's at work, and I'm stuck in this big house on a gorgeous day. I won't be any trouble. Scout's honor."

I wasn't keen on the idea, but saying "no" might have made me a male Neanderthal. So I told her I had a little research to do in town first and that she could meet me at Lyle's library if she wanted. The invitation was not overly warm, and I had reason to hope she'd not show up.

It was still spring-like outside, almost convertible weather, as I drove into Lyle heading toward the library. Lyle's library, a county facility, had a decent research room. I worked my way through newspaper accounts of Reilly's career, how he first sang on a Winchester radio talent show and lost. The accounts varied, but it seemed he was too blue, melancholy, or deep, whatever that meant. The winner of the talent show was a church group. In any case, a Nashville record producer was driving the Skyline Drive, heard the station, and signed Reilly to a contract.

What I was searching for was the connection between Reilly and someone named Hollinger. As Chester indicated, a Courtney Hollinger had been arrested in Tyler City for "assault on a white woman and the murder of the man that came to her aid." Courtney was black. Five days later, Courtney was found dead in his cell. He had "hanged himself rather than face justice."

The white woman's name wasn't mentioned nor were details of the assault. I had doubts that the Hollinger mentioned in the articles had anything to do with Reilly. I never heard him say anything that sounded racially biased. Nor had I heard him say anything that suggested he was active in fighting prejudice. Reilly was either color neutral or indifferent.

Amy found me at the library. "The lady at the front desk told me where you were. Learn anything interesting?"

"Not really. Let's find out what Jeb Garrett has to say about Reilly and the poor farm."

"Who's Jeb Garrett?" asked Amy.

"An attorney who worked for Reilly. If anyone would know if Reilly had plans to sell the poor farm, he's the guy."

A cloud crossed Amy's face. She managed a smile. "By all means, let's ask him."

Chapter 14

Front Royal borders the South Fork of the Shenandoah River. The river is an anomaly in that it flows from south to north. The town itself is an anomaly because there doesn't seem to be much of a reason why it's still there. John Marshall used to live nearby. The entrance to the Skyline Drive, a beautiful road that runs along the top of the Blue Ridge Mountains, is here, but that's hardly a reason for setting up housekeeping.

In more recent times, the EPA closed the textile plant on the west side of town, removing the source of the town's smelly air as well as a major source of employment. And yet the town seemed to be thriving. Maybe towns, like murders, don't always need reasons.

After driving in circles for a few minutes, a gas station attendant directed me to a street a block from the courthouse. I found Jeb's office above an antique store, his name painted on the window outside. I was reminded of an old movie I saw in prison with Humphrey Bogart, but I couldn't remember which one. Bogie movies were very popular in prison.

I thought Amy would check out the antique store. Instead, she followed me up the stairs to Jeb's office. We stepped into a small waiting room. No one was minding the receptionist's desk. If it weren't for a nameplate, I would have assumed that no one had sat there for a long time. The desk was clean. No calendar, pictures, yellow stickies. Not even a paper clip. I picked up the nameplate. The brass was shiny, the words "Lydia Thatcher, Paralegal" etched into the metal in script.

The door to Jeb's office was closed, but I could hear music coming from inside. I knocked lightly, then opened the door. Jeb was at his desk eating. I knocked louder and he looked up. He scrambled to put down his sandwich and shut off the CD player.

"I'm sorry," he said standing. He wiped his hands on a napkin, and we shook hands. "Jeb Garrett," he said in a deep voice. "You must be Mr. Harrington. I apologize for not hearing you come in, but my receptionist is out sick."

Jeb was not your stereotypical lawyer. A few inches over six feet tall, with a long beard and a bear's body, he was dressed in jeans and plaid shirt. I suspected he snacked often. I introduced Amy as my assistant, which drew a flash of a smile from Jeb. I suspected he'd had a few assistants, too.

His office was washed with light from a long row of windows and three large skylights. Most horizontal surfaces were occupied with books and stacks of papers, but in an ordered sort of way. In response to the warm weather, a door leading to an outside set of stairs had been propped open with a legal dictionary. That was the first time I actually saw a lawyer use one of those.

"I'm a beneficiary of Reilly Heartwood's will," I said shaking Jeb's hand. "I've apparently inherited the poor farm. I have a few questions about Reilly and his plans for the farm."

"I can't tell you anything about my client or his affairs."

"I understand that, but you agreed to this meeting, and I

had hoped you could simply relate to me whether or not Reilly spoke to you about selling the farm."

Jeb shook his head. "Sorry, I'm compelled by a code of ethics to maintain the secrecy of my communications with my client. I'm sure you can appreciate that."

"Could you tell me if you ever talked to Tom Stewart?"

I heard Amy gasp. I hadn't thought about the question before asking it.

"I haven't," said Jeb impatiently. "What makes you think I have?"

"Nothing. His clients want to buy the farm from me, that's all."

"I'd like to help," said Jeb, walking me to the door, "but I'm afraid there's nothing I can do until I have a letter from the executor of the estate and proof of qualification. I'll be leaving tomorrow evening for the holidays, so maybe you should come back after the first of the year."

I checked Amy. Her demeanor had gone from surprise at the mention of Tom to obvious suppressed rage. Traveling with her was like sitting next to a grenade, not knowing if the pin had been pulled. I asked Jeb if I might use the phone. I called Robbie, who assured me she'd promptly get Sarah qualified, and have her sign a letter to get Jeb talking. In turn, I convinced Jeb to meet me again before he left.

By the time we reached the car, Amy was fuming. "You no good son-of-a-bitch! You're thinking about selling the poor farm. I thought you were different. I thought you cared about people. You're just like Tom. How could I have been so stupid?!"

I tried to console her, but she'd have none of it. "I have to go home," she said.

"No problem," I said, opening the car door.

"Not with you."

"Amy, please."

"Fuck you," she said, and walked away.

I let the irony pass, and I let her walk away without further pleading. To be honest, her departure was a relief.

With Amy gone, I was free to speculate about why Tom might have killed Reilly. My theory was that Tom had done so in a fit of anger. After he killed Reilly, he sent Amy back to Reilly's house to make sure Reilly hadn't left something behind that would implicate Tom in Reilly's murder. I couldn't think of what that something might be, nor could I see Amy helping him, but no theory based on pure speculation is perfect.

In Tom's favor was the fact that Reilly's death wasn't going to attract a serious investigation. A lot of folks were still bitter that he didn't make them rich. The sheriff wasn't going to investigate the crime because he assumed the finger of guilt would point at one of the town folk. Reilly's murder was a perfect crime because Reilly was a perfect victim: people wanted him dead and were not fussy about how it happened.

That was my theory, and I was proud of it. All I had to do was prove it.

I decided to test my theory on Cali McBride. I found the offices of the Valley Post, Front Royal's oldest continuously published newspaper and Cali's employer. A withered old man with a nest of snow-white hair met me at the front desk. I asked him for Cali and he disappeared.

The walls of the reception area were lined with old newspapers. A paper from 1862 ran the banner: "Yankees Fire on Front Royal, Picnic Ruined." Below the headline was the caption: "Visitors From the North Hanged."

I heard someone enter the room. The voice seemed to come from my head. Sweet. Soft. A touch of an accent. I loved her voice. "May I help you?"

I turned and looked at Cali, hoping I wasn't giving off signals about my one-night stand with Amy. "Catch any serial killers?" I asked.

"No," replied Cali, "but I learned some things."

I pretended to be distracted by a hangnail. "Would you like to share them with me?"

Cali replied, "Not really. But I'll trade what I learned and will learn about Courtney Hollinger and Reilly for everything you know and will know about Reilly's murder."

"I see."

"And I want an exclusive interview with you."

"Jesus," I said. "The next thing you'll want to do is go to lunch."

"I know just the place."

We went to a Greek restaurant and Cali ordered. The waiter brought course after course of dishes I couldn't pronounce, and we ate them all. Coffee came and I asked Cali again about her past. She focused her big greens on me. "Okay. Here's the deal. I'm working at the Valley Post because I had a problem with a source in Chicago. I was working on a story about corruption and my informant mentioned names. I believed him, and the paper printed the story, only the source, it turned out, was using me to discredit others. I also had a few personal problems to deal with. Then I tried to get back into reporting. This was the only job I could find. I've written about lost cats, weddings, azalea festivals, and funerals. I've learned a lot, but I want a story that'll challenge me. I want to write about Reilly. And I want to write your story."

"I don't have a story," I said.

"Come on. You were tried on television and sent to jail in front of millions of viewers. Three years later, you're free and no one says a word. I know there's a story there. I mean, what's it like to be in prison for something you didn't do? How do you feel about the money the government pays you for your lost time?"

I laughed. "The government doesn't pay you for your time. The maximum recovery from the feds is five thousand dollars. In most states, prisoners released after years on death row get nothing unless the legislature gives it to 'em."

"See? That's compelling. Most people don't know that and would be fascinated to read it. I know the big magazines and television news programs followed your trial. It's got to hurt that no one cared enough to call after you were vindicated and released. I know it would piss me off. So here's your chance to have your story told. Bottom line? I need a break and you need my help."

"Maybe," I said.

"Okay. As a gesture of good faith, this is what I've found out so far." She handed me copies of two articles. The first was a front-page article about a homicide at the county fair. Courtney Hollinger, "a Negro," had been arrested in a fight with a white man named Randy Harris. According to the article, Courtney had been harassing a woman when Randy Harris came to her aid. In the scuffle, Harris hit his head on a picnic table and died. The suspect was taken to the Tyler Town jail.

The second article was buried on page ten. Cali read it to me. "Courtney Hollinger, the alleged killer of Randy Harris, was found dead in his jail cell. According to Sheriff Steele, Hollinger hanged himself with a bed sheet. Deputy Henry Midgett said he heard nothing unusual during the evening. He found the body as he made his usual check of the prisoners."

"The deputy's name was Midgett?"

"Right. It's a common name in North Carolina. A small group of Midgetts lives here in Front Royal." She laughed. "That came out funny, but you know what I mean. Now I tried to find out the identity of the white woman, but her name wasn't mentioned in the paper. I know some people at the courthouse in Tyler Town, so I should be able to get that information tomorrow. I did learn that Courtney's father was a preacher at a church not far from here. Courtney's father is dead, but the new minister had heard stories about Reilly helping out, like when the church caught fire. So I'm going to talk to him tomorrow. If you want to know what happened to Courtney Hollinger, you need me. And I need you. What could be simpler?"

I hesitated because I didn't want to be thrust back into the public's eye. But the government had promised me a public apology that had never come. I didn't trust the mega-media. I didn't want to be portrayed as some whiny putz who blamed others for his mistakes. And yet I wanted the record set straight. Thanks to Reilly, I had more than enough money. I no longer needed what my old company and the government had agreed to pay me. "We need to talk about limits to what you write about me."

She patted her lips with her napkin. "And you still need to tell me all you know about the murder of Reilly Heartwood."

Chapter 15

*A*s I drove back to Lyle, the last rays of the sun were slipping behind the Blue Ridge mountains. Cali had listened to my theory about how Tom killed Reilly in a pique of rage. She then proceeded to poke holes in it. I couldn't explain how killing Reilly would have benefited Tom. I had no good explanation why Amy would help him. And I couldn't explain Doc's behavior other than the fact that he was an old man who was incompetent.

The conversation turned to my relationship with Reilly. I ended up telling Cali my life story, starting with my first memories as a child until the day I was arrested. Lunch stretched into the afternoon, the time in her company passing quickly. If it had been up to her, I would have gone on longer, but I pleaded exhaustion.

⌇

On my arrival at Reilly's house, I found Frieda waiting for me, a grim look on her face. "I was wondering where you disappeared to. We've got to get this house in order for the viewing tomorrow. Food has to be prepared. The cats have to be taken care of."

I had no doubt that all of this had already been done and

then done again. Frieda was complaining because she was worried about where I was and whether I was holding a grudge from our morning tiff. "You're absolutely right," I said. "What can I do to help?"

"You can stay out of the way is what you can do," she answered. "And you can get Lora Jean to feed these cats."

"And where is LJ at this moment?"

"I think she's in the study. I told her not to go in there, but she just rolled her eyes. She said you were in there so she could go in there too. Young people!"

Frieda sighed, allowed herself to look peeved for a moment, then said in her usual demanding tone: "I know you haven't eaten enough. You can't live on beer and peanuts. I'm going to make you something hot and you're going to eat it."

I was still full from lunch, but knew better than to say that. "Thank you, Frieda," I said gratefully.

"With Lora Jean sick and your not eating, it's enough to drive me crazy. I'm not going to be responsible if you get Lora Jean's cold."

"I feel fine," I said. "Everything's under control." It wasn't, but the words sounded good.

"I'm doing what I can. That's all I can do," she said. At least Frieda was back to normal.

I went to the study. The door was open, and I heard the familiar sound of computer-generated gunfire. I found Lora Jean staring at the monitor blowing holes in a tank.

"Hey," I said.

Lora Jean jumped and her helicopter was blown to pieces. "Now look what you did," she said, then in a softer tone, "You scared me."

"Sorry." A second passed before I realized the significance of what I was looking at. "How did you get past the security screen?" She looked puzzled. "The computer comes on," I added, "and asks for a password."

Lora Jean shook her head. "It said to enter password, so I typed the word password. Did I do something wrong?"

Reilly had taken the prompt literally. Lora Jean had done the same. I might have spent hours trying to crack Reilly's computer. All I had to do was what the machine asked, and the computer's files would have been accessible.

"Not at all. Frieda wants you to feed the cats and take your medicine. I need to use the computer. But first, I need to ask you a question." She gave me a worried teen-age look. "I found another note on my car last night. I was wondering if you had your school yearbooks here."

"I have them upstairs."

"Would you mind if I looked through them?"

She answered with a scowl. "Yeah. I mean, I've got personal stuff in there."

"Okay. How about if you flip the pages and only show me the class pictures?"

"I'll get them," she said in a defeated tone. "Is Reilly ever going to have a funeral?"

"I'm working on it, LJ."

"But you'll have to apologize to Rose," she said. "Doc and Frieda were arguing about it. Why can't Reilly just be buried like everyone else? I mean, whatever Reilly did or your mom did, why can't people just forget it? It was like a long time ago." She shook her head. "Kids are always being told to forget things. The whole thing just seems dumb."

Hearing it from Lora Jean, it did seem dumb.

"Maybe you have a point."

The recognition brought a smile to her face. "I'll be right back."

Frieda appeared with the cordless phone. "Mr. Garrett's on the line."

"This is Shep Harrington."

Jeb came on the line. "A courier called and the papers should be here this evening. I would like to meet with you this evening if possible so I can get an early start on my vacation tomorrow. How about nine at my office?"

I told him I'd be there. I thanked him and hung up. At least I would know for certain what Reilly was planning on doing with the poor farm. A small victory, but one I was happy to have. I called Cali and told her about my meeting. She agreed to meet me at Jeb's office.

LJ returned and we went into the dining room. "I need you to help me identify a kid in town," I said. "He's been following me. I only got a glimpse of him, so you're going to have to make your best guess of who it might be."

"Shouldn't be too hard," replied Lora Jean. "Our school's not that big."

Lora Jean was only a sophomore. I had no idea how old the kid was and whether Lora Jean would even know him. "That's Mary Beth," said Lora Jean. "Her and me were best friends until last Wednesday." I resisted the impulse to correct her grammar and let her flip the pages. Lora Jean alternated between offering me possibilities and giving me a running commentary on the student body. We came to the end of the pictures with no match.

"Let's try this one more time. The boy I'm looking for likes to slick his hair back."

"Which boy doesn't?"

I thought again about the boy I'd seen in the Bowlarama parking lot. "And he's tall and wears black motorcycle boots."

"With a metal toe?"

I replayed the image of the boy running from the light to the shadows. "Yeah. Now that you mention it."

Lora Jean shook her head. "You didn't say anything about boots." She pointed to a picture of a boy with short hair and a broad smile. "Is that him?"

My first impulse was to say no way. The face was too innocent, too happy. Then I imagined the boy with long hair and fire in his eyes. "It could be. Who is he?"

"That's Rodney Tierney," said Lora Jean.

The name "Rodney" made me think of Peyton Place. During a two-month stretch, the movie was played every night in the prison library. One prisoner got so tired of it, he ripped it from the VCR and destroyed the tape. He lost his privileges for a while, but to a lot of us, he was a hero.

I glanced at Lora Jean. It was improbable that she knew anything of Peyton Place, but I saw the worry in her eyes. To me, Rodney was a piece of a puzzle. I didn't care if Rodney was involved or not, but it mattered to Lora Jean.

She made a face. "Is Rodney in trouble?"

"Not with me," I said. "I just need to talk to him."

Lora Jean nodded. "He lives with his mother and his grandfather, Mr. Potter. Mr. Potter used to be nice when Rodney was young, but not anymore. I think Mr. Potter beats Rodney's mom and hit Rodney until he got too big. Rodney hates him." She looked at the photograph. "Rodney used to be a happy kid."

I looked at the picture with consternation. My only suspect was Tom Stewart. I liked it that way. Yet I was receiving threats from the grandson of one of the men ruined by Reilly's decision to leave town. Another fact, another question.

"Thanks LJ," I said. "You've been a big help."

Frieda appeared with her hands on her hip. "You can look at yearbooks later. I've got dinner ready and we're going to eat it while it's hot."

The three of us went into the kitchen. Frieda left only after watching Lora Jean swallow an antibiotic and making sure I ate a large helping of chicken stuffed with rice and mushrooms. She took Lora Jean home. Both would be back in the morning for the viewing.

I rebooted the computer and on the prompt, typed the word "PASSWORD." There were chortling sounds as the code was processed, then a menu of five options scrolled onto the screen: CORPORATE ACCOUNTS, INDIVIDUAL ACCOUNTS, ROY-ALTIES, PORTFOLIO, GAMES.

I clicked on individual accounts and was presented with another menu, this one a list of names, including people mentioned in the will, townspeople, the residents of the poor farm, and people I didn't know. To my surprise, one of Reilly's companies owned the bowling alley where Chester worked. And, according to the computer file, the bowling alley had operated at a loss for nearly a decade. I scanned some other accounts and discovered that through various companies and foundations, Reilly had been giving money to many Lyle people who didn't know it or didn't care to admit it.

I leaned back in the chair and drummed my fingers on the desk. Reilly was a stubborn and proud man. He hadn't done anything to the people of Lyle. To publicly repay the investors in the studio would be an admission that he had. But Reilly wasn't going to leave them broke either. I suspected he naively thought they'd eventually realize that the collapse of the studio deal wasn't his fault. People, unfortunately, don't relinquish blaming rights that easily. How much pain did Reilly endure waiting for these folks to embrace him? How hard was it for him to hear the old lies whispered by the new residents of Lyle? Enough to shoot himself?

I turned away from these thoughts and returned to the computer files. Of all the beneficiaries, one name that stood out was Darrel Potter. He had been getting payments until about five months ago. I searched the computer to see if I could determine why he been cut off, but found nothing.

An hour of staring at numbers on a computer screen was as much as I could endure. My interest waned, my eyelids fluttered, and my brain was shutting down. I went into the living room and lay down on the couch a few feet away from Reilly. I closed my eyes, confident my nap would be shorter than his. But sleep wouldn't come. I sat up and rubbed my eyes. Darrel Potter's file was annoying me. I was comfortable with my theory pegging Tom as Reilly's killer, yet I knew Darrel not only had a temper but had harbored a grudge against Reilly for many years. Cutting off payments to Darrel might have been enough to send Darrel into a homicidal rage, especially if he'd been drinking. In many ways, Darrel was the most logical candidate for the crime. I needed to talk to him face-to-face.

჻

Darrel Potter's house was a few blocks away from the last of the renovated houses, not far from my mother's childhood home. Even in the moonlight, the house had the look of a comatose patient: functional in the clinical sense, but not alive. Gutters hung loosely from the roof. The railing around the porch was broken. And light fixtures were twisted at random angles. This soiled nest was the ugly duckling in a neighborhood of tidy blockhouses, all of the same design. The others had been treated with paint and trim and imagination, the common denominator seeming to be plastic geese, ducks, and sunflowers, a motif that actually seemed charming. Most houses were adorned with Christmas lights. A few had Santas and reindeer in elaborate formations.

But not at Darrel's house. Darrel's house was dark and gloomy, more suited for Halloween than Christmas.

I parked the car on the street and walked slowly up the driveway. I had just reached the sidewalk when the front door of the house opened and a gaunt, bent man stepped off the front porch. He limped slightly and his left arm seemed to dangle from his shoulder. In his right hand, he held a cigarette that trembled ever so slightly as he brought it to his lips. Darrel was a lot like his house.

"You're Mary's son," he said quietly. I nodded. "I heard you were in town asking questions about how Reilly died." His voice lacked enough force to convey whether he was asking a question or merely reminding himself of something he knew.

"Is Rodney here?" I asked.

Darrel shook his head. "Would you hang around here if you were eighteen?" He sucked on his cigarette and coughed. "Is the boy in trouble?"

It was the second time I had been asked that question. To my surprise, there was concern in Darrel's voice. "I don't know, Mr. Potter. It's possible he thinks he is, or maybe he thinks you are."

"Ain't likely anyone knows what the boy thinks."

"Any idea why he might be following me? Why he might want to scare me into leaving town?"

"Not a clue," replied Darrel, in a deep smoker's voice. "Got a mind of his own."

I nodded, then said: "Could you tell me where you were on the night Reilly died?"

Darrel looked away. "Reilly invited some folks to his house that night. I invited myself. Got there early." He inhaled a lung full of smoke, then coughed it out. "Reilly wasn't glad to see me. I told him I'd fallen off the wagon and needed a little assistance to reconstitute my investment portfolio. He wasn't interested. Told me that he'd done enough to help me, that if I couldn't help myself by now, I should beat it." Darrel spit a fleck of tobacco off his tongue. "The man was a prick. I spent the rest of the evening at home."

"What time did you return here?"

"I arrived at about 6:30." I gave him a blank look. "Ask my

daughter. I believe I hit her at about 6:35."

"Your alibi is that you were beating your daughter?"

"I wouldn't put it quite that way, but yeah. So what?" Darrel shook his head. "You city folk always got to judge everyone." Darrel turned and dragged himself inside.

I constructed a new theory. Darrel Potter comes after Reilly for a handout, and when he's turned down, he comes home and smacks his daughter. He gets drunk, then goes back and kills Reilly. Rodney knows it and wants to scare me off. I considered this for a moment. I knew I wouldn't be able to prove it. His daughter would say he was home at the time Reilly checked out. I shook my head. "Just like the Waltons," I said out loud, then headed back to my car.

Chapter 16

It was 7:00 p.m. when I got back to Reilly's house. I sat in the sunroom and sipped a soda. The more I learned about Reilly's death, the less, it seemed, I knew. The paradox went this way: if I accepted the story that Reilly committed suicide, then I knew who killed him. But if Gus and Zak concluded that Reilly had been murdered, I wouldn't know who killed him, so I would know less. The more I learned about people who might have had a motive to kill Reilly, the less certain I became that any one of them was the killer. I couldn't recall Columbo having these problems.

My brain was stuck on this mental merry-go-round when the phone rang. I thought it might be Amy, but she usually didn't bother to knock or call. The caller, to my surprise, was Tom Stewart. "I'd like to speak with you." Before I could respond, he asked, "Is Amy there? I know she's been visiting with you."

I wasn't sure exactly what he knew about last night's visit, but I deflected the issue by answering, "No."

He seemed distressed, even worried. "If you don't mind, could you meet me in town?"

I suggested the coffee bar. Ten minutes later, I was sucking on a mocha double espresso supreme. Tom satisfied himself by chewing on a hangnail.

"I'm sure Amy has told you that she's filed for divorce."

"She mentioned it."

Tom stopped gnawing on his finger and leaned back. "God, she'll tell anyone who'll listen how terribly she's been treated."

"I don't need to be involved in all of this," I said.

"But you are involved, Mr. Harrington. What you heard from my wife is that I've lost the family fortune betting on land deals, that I've thrown families into the cold, and that I intend to do the same with the folks at the poor farm. I'm supposed to be the driven attorney who doesn't care if old people eat dog food as long as my clients can buy the homestead and sell it for a profit." He shook his head. "I've heard the story many times."

I reminded Tom of what he'd said at lunch.

"I was needling her. I had just read her attorney's latest settlement proposal, and I wanted to get back at her. It was a tacky thing to do, but I was pissed!"

For the moment, I saw Tom not as the arrogant attorney but as a beaten dog.

"I was a real estate attorney when Amy and I got married. I made a good living, but not like others in the firm. Amy was surrounded by women who didn't have to work, who could afford big houses and people to attend to them. She pushed me to go into commercial real estate ventures. She could look at a property and see its potential. I was amazed at first. But her penchant for the end game blinded her to the details. She was ruthless when it came to business. On a human level, the consequences of real estate development can be devastating. Most people in the business deal with the human problems first, or they don't do the deal. That's not a humanitarian response, but good business. Amy saw only her objective, like pilots who bomb from thirty thousand feet but don't see the collateral damage. But when she was confronted with the pain we'd caused individuals, she couldn't handle the guilt. I didn't know that she'd fought mental problems all of her life. I guess that sounds uncaring. If I had, maybe I could have been a little more aware. I don't know. Now she pops pills. She's been to Betty Ford a few times, but the treatment doesn't last. Every so often, she decides to leave me and hires a lawyer." Tom's voice cracked and he cleared his throat. "One of these times she'll leave and not come back."

I sipped my coffee and let him regain his composure. After a moment, I said, "You don't need to explain this to me, Mr. Stewart. I believe I understand that Amy has problems."

"Amy's not well. I'm sure you know that, but you may not understand how ill she is and how it affects her. Did she show you the burn on her arm?"

"She may have," I said. I was not ready to trust Tom.

"She probably told you that I did it to her. The truth is that, in my presence, she burned herself to prove I had no power over her." He shook his head and ran his hands through his hair. "She's very complex, Mr. Harrington."

"I don't mean to be rude," I said, "but I have an appointment this evening. I don't think you asked me here to talk about your wife."

"I'll get right to the point. I represent the owners of the land adjacent to the poor farm. I took the business because Robbie asked me to. I never realized how my association with this sale would affect Amy, but it's caused her to relapse—the pills, the drinking, the divorce proceedings."

"I'm sorry," I said. "You said you wanted to come to the point. Maybe I missed it."

"The point is that Amy is trying to convince you that I killed Reilly or that one of my clients did. She doesn't want me to close this deal because she's convinced the residents of the farm will be evicted and she'll be blamed for it. I've tried to convince her that the residents would all be taken care of, but she won't listen. I would like to facilitate the purchase of the poor farm for my clients. I have no interest in this transaction other than my fee. I'd like to discuss with you the ways we might handle the residents so that they're not unduly inconvenienced and have what they need."

"I told you, I'll do what Reilly would have done."

"But we don't know what he'd do, do we? The day before he died, he told me he'd consider my last offer and call me. He didn't call me because he didn't have the chance."

"Or maybe he just was tired of talking about it." I was.

Tom stood up. "Thank you for your time, Mr. Harrington," he said, but didn't leave. "I have one other request," he said, his eyes becoming glassy. "I would appreciate it if you wouldn't sleep with my wife again. I understand what happened. I mean, you're not the first. But I'd prefer that you not take advantage of her a second time."

Staring into the eyes of a man who's asking you not to have sex with his wife is awkward to say the least. But Tom wasn't threatening me or even angry. He looked hurt, like a man hopelessly in love with a woman who was beyond reciprocating his passion. I had taken a big leap from thinking of Tom as a murder suspect to feeling sorry for him. Whether I continued in my sympathetic mode depended on whether Tom's story hung together. One of the Stewarts was lying. I just didn't know which one.

Tom stared at me through sad, tired eyes. "Call me if you want to hear my proposal on the poor farm," he said. He stepped toward the door, then turned back. "Oh, I forgot to tell you. I'm sorry about Reilly. He was a nice man."

"Thanks," I said. I watched my former favorite murder suspect leave, wondering if he was really a sap or just a good actor.

I arrived in Front Royal a little before nine. The lights to Jeb's office were out, and I wondered if I'd arrived too early or if Jeb had changed his mind. I waited a few minutes for Cali, then headed up the stairs. I tried the outer door to his office and found it unlocked. I called out, but there was no answer. Moonlight filled the reception area with shadows and dark shapes. I listened for a moment, but all I heard was the thumping of my own heart. My flight reflex is well tuned, and the smart thing to do would have been to let my innate good sense take me back to my car. But I was drawn to the source of the light—Jeb's open door.

I stepped inside, my apprehension rising. Papers were scattered everywhere. His chair was on its side. A foot extended from behind the desk. I stepped toward the windows and froze. His massive body was crumpled against the wall, his face up, his eyes open and fixed in a death stare. The right side of his face glistened in the soft light.

I crouched over him and touched his neck. He was still warm, but he had no pulse. I hesitated, my instincts confused by the contradiction of a warm but lifeless body. I stood up looking for the phone on Jeb's desk when I caught a glimpse of a shadowy form coming toward me.

Then I felt something hard against my skull. Lightening flashed across my eyes. I put my arms up, only to be hit again. I was barely vertical when another blow glanced off the left side of my head. I fell backwards, landing on my side. I rolled away from my ghostly pursuer and tried to stand once again.

The fact was, I only imagined getting to my feet. I was actually face down on the floor, gripped by the realization that the next hit would send me into sleep I was never going to escape.

But instead of the crack of my skull, I heard a familiar voice. The angel of death had been spooked by the angel of mercy—Cali. I needed to warn her, but I couldn't make myself speak. I felt two fingers on my neck, then drifted into darkness.

I didn't want to open my eyes. People were calling my name and asking me over and over if I could hear them. I said yes once and tried to look at them, only to be rewarded with shooting pains that made me feel like throwing up. I wasn't excited about doing that again.

The voice that changed my mind belonged to Cali McBride. This time I opened one eye a little. The lights had been turned down, but I saw her hovering over me. I raised my right arm to touch her face and another shot of pain gripped me. "Easy," she said.

A woman dressed in white arrived holding a clipboard. "No broken bones," she said. "A couple of bumps on his head. It could have been a lot worse. We'll keep him overnight for observation to be safe."

"Where am I?" I asked.

"Memorial Hospital in Front Royal," said Cali.

I opened both eyes. "I want to go home."

"You need to be where someone can watch you," said Cali.

I noticed the state trooper hovering behind Cali.

"What's *he* doing here?" I asked.

"Until a few minutes ago, he was guarding you," said Cali softly. I loved her voice. She could have told me they amputated my leg and it wouldn't have mattered. "An ex-felon found at the scene of a murder is at least suspicious, if not a suspect. I told them about your friend Gus and he vouched for you, so you don't have to worry about the police for now. He'll take a statement, then you can get some rest, some soft food, and get better."

"I can't stay here," I said, taking her hand. "It's too much like being locked up." It was a pathetic display, but I was truly afraid to spend the night at the hospital. "Please?"

Cali studied me for a moment, then turned to the lady with the clipboard. "Are you a doctor?"

"A nurse practitioner," replied the woman a bit defensively.

"Tell me what to watch for, and I'll take him home."

The N.P. made a face. "I hope you know what you're volunteering for. He's going to be a bear or a baby when the pain sets in." Cali just looked at the N.P., who rolled her eyes. Then the N.P. handed me two pills. "Swallow these. They'll knock the edge off the pain until you get home. I'll get the discharge papers, but you'll have to sign a waiver."

Cali helped me sit up. My stomach did a few cartwheels. Cali must have noticed I was feeling queasy and handed me an icepack. I mopped my face with it and the nausea passed.

"I saw a movie where the girl kissed the guy on the places

it hurt and the pain went away," I said.

A smile appeared on Cali's face. She put her hand on my cheek and said softly, "I'm tired and you smell like barf and disinfectant. Not to mention I don't know you as well as I know my mailman, and I'm not putting out for him either."

Her hand lingered for a moment, and I pressed it against my face. For a moment, the reality of what happened and what could have happened overwhelmed me. And yet, despite the demons from prison, and the dark empties that I had endured, all of my fears were held at bay by the touch of a woman I barely knew. If Reilly's death had a silver lining, it was my meeting Cali and feeling the contentment that comes from trusting someone again.

A man who looked like he'd seen too many cheeseburgers appeared, introduced himself as "Detective Somebody," and asked if I was up to giving a statement. I told him about the phone call, my appointment, and finding Jeb.

I signed something and the cop left. An orderly came in with a wheelchair and the N.P. showed up with a handful of papers. "Read it and sign it," she said, then looking at Cali, "and you sign as a witness."

I looked at the three pages of small type and marveled at how many words it took the hospital lawyer to construct a wall high enough to keep my lawyer from getting into the hospital's insurance. I signed dutifully and so did Cali. Then the orderly signed and the N.P. signed.

The orderly handed me a shirt. "They cut your shirt off when they brought you in. I had this in my locker. You can keep it."

The man smiled at me. "You should've been a doctor," I

said. "Thanks. And Merry Christmas."

Cali helped me with the shirt. We gave up trying to put my right arm through the sleeve. She buttoned the front and I slipped off the bed. To my relief, my head had cleared some. Cali went to get her car, and the orderly wheeled me to the entrance.

He handed me a kidney shaped dish. "In case you get sick," he said. As he helped me to my feet and then into Cali's car, I took the dish.

Cali drove to Lyle, her eyes darting from the road to me. "I'm really okay," I said.

"You scared me to death," she said, then adding, "your friend Reilly is—was—a very complicated man."

She hit a pothole and I stifled a yelp. "Did you find out something?"

"Funny you should ask. Courtney Hollinger's relatives left the area a long time ago. I found the church where he was buried and checked with the current minister, a man named Samuel Jones. He's too young to have met Courtney so I didn't find out anything useful about him."

I took a long, slow breath. "But you found out something?"

"Are you sure you're up for this?"

I wasn't, but I said I was.

"Preacher Jones had heard about C.C. Hollinger. Apparently, C.C. Hollinger made a significant donation to rebuild the church after a suspicious fire destroyed it. Preacher Jones said he later learned that C.C. Hollinger was Reilly's stage name. Anyway, Reilly, or Hollinger, made the donation on the condition that he remain an anonymous contributor."

"So Preacher Jones tells a newspaper reporter?"

"He thought now that Reilly was dead, someone should know. But none of this is important. Preacher Jones told me that he found a box of letters in the rectory that included letters from a man calling himself C.C. Hollinger. Hollinger addressed the letters to the former preacher. Reverend Jones said he gave the box to the sister of the former preacher. Her name is Mattie Devereaux, and she is still in the area. I think we should look at those letters. The Reverend Jones is trying to arrange a visit with her tomorrow afternoon."

"Impressive," I said. I didn't understand all of what Cali said, but it sounded good.

"Thanks," said Cali, clearly pleased with herself. She glanced at me several times. "I guess I could have picked a better time to unload on you."

"I'm fine. I'm just sorry for imposing on you."

"You're my story," said Cali. "I have to take care of you. To be honest, it's been a while since I've felt useful. I don't mind, really."

I heard sadness in her voice, along with a tremor of excitement. To my ears, it sounded like an invitation to see if we might be friends. Unfortunately, Cali's timing couldn't have been worse. I felt for the barf dish with my left hand. A cold chill ran down my back, and then the heaves came. I wretched for about five minutes, then leaned back in the seat. "Sorry. This is not my idea of a first date."

"We should have a second so we can laugh about the first," she said.

Chapter 17

Awakening after being beaten to a pulp is a lot like waking up after drinking all night. If you lie still enough, you can pretend you feel okay. I had been struck in the ribs, the forearm several times, and the head twice. But the moment I opened my eyes, I actually felt pretty good. A little headache, but manageable. But, as with a hangover, one move, even a deep breath, is often enough to allow reality to return. I coughed and everything hurt—ribs, arm, head—all at once. I took solace that I was alive to feel the pain, then wondered how it was that I hadn't been killed. I had escaped with bruises and a few knots on my head while poor Jeb had been beaten to death. Same weapon. Same attacker. I considered this for a moment, then rolled out of bed. I wasn't ready to answer this new set of questions just yet.

My solution to everything is a long hot shower. Thirty minutes of steam and heat and four ibuprofens and I actually managed to shave, dress myself, and walk downstairs.

The foyer was a busy place. Men in suits were setting up two parallel lines of stanchions linked with velvet cables. A red carpet was laid between them. I spoke with one of the men long enough to learn that Sarah had hired them. I followed the carpet into the living room past Reilly's coffin to a door that led to a patio outside the house. Some of the men were busy packing up anything that could be concealed—ashtrays, books, and vases. Others were putting up a plastic panel in front of the coffin. I must have appeared puzzled by this activity because one of the men explained the process without my asking. "Grieving fans are not above taking souvenirs, including body parts," he said. If I was going to have to apologize to Rose to get Reilly buried, it was comforting to know that at least I was going to be burying all of him.

I found Frieda in the kitchen staring into a cup of coffee. To my surprise and relief, she wasn't cooking. Even *she* couldn't serve the throngs of fans who were gathering to pay homage to C.C. Hollinger. She looked up at me, but said nothing. No rush to mother me, no gentle scolding either. Just sad, bewildered eyes.

She looked away, pressing her fingers to her temples. "You could've been killed! I don't understand what's happening. I don't know what to do or think anymore. I don't know what I'm doing here or where I'm supposed to go."

"Everything will work out," I said.

Frieda brought her hand down hard on the table, spilling her coffee. "You don't know that. You don't know what's going to happen next. So don't tell me that everything's going to be fine. You'll go home soon. Maybe everything will be fine for you." She covered her face and sobbed.

I suppose I should have comforted her, but I didn't have the energy. I was weary of dealing with the people Reilly left behind, including myself. I almost didn't give a damn about what happened to anyone. Then Lora Jean appeared. She looked at Frieda, the spilled coffee, and seemed to sense the tension in the air. Then she looked at me. "Gus and that creepy guy, Zak, are in the study," she said softly. "They told me to wake you up."

"Thanks LJ."

I poured a cup of coffee. I carried it in my left hand and managed to spill half of it before I got out of the kitchen. Frieda said she'd clean it up, that I should go talk to my friends.

The morning had started well.

Gus and Zak were hovering over the couch where Reilly died. As I got closer to them, I saw a dummy sitting where Reilly had been shot. The dummy's extended right leg was resting on a pillow atop the coffee table. A rod went through the dummy's chest and out the back. Zak was using a protractor to adjust the angle. I was relieved that Reilly was no longer playing the part of victim.

"Good to see you among the living," said Gus. "You were lucky."

I touched my head. "Yeah. A lot luckier than Jeb Garrett."

Zak stuffed half a donut into his mouth and washed it down with coffee. He took a file folder from a briefcase and handed it to me. "This is the preliminary report on Jeb Garrett. I'll spare you the photographs. He was killed by repeated blows to the head with a kid's aluminum baseball bat. Do you get it?"

"Get *what?*" I tried to find some significance in using a metal bat as a weapon, but nothing came to mind.

"Repeated blows," said Zak, "means that no single blow was sufficient to do the job."

"And that means?"

Gus said, "It may mean nothing. Or it may tell us that his assailant wasn't strong enough to kill him with one blow."

"Maybe," said Zak, "or maybe the killer was timid about hitting another person. Perhaps the killer knew him." He took a sip of coffee and waited for my reaction.

"Then what about me?" I asked. "Did the killer know me as well? Wouldn't that be too coincidental?"

Zak shrugged. "Just speculating," he said with a hint of defensiveness. Zak liked to be right. "Anyway, both your blood type and Jeb's blood type were found on the end of the bat, suggesting that you were a victim and not a perp."

I looked at the couch and at Reilly's surrogate. "And what's your theory about how Reilly died?"

"Bottom line," said Gus, "is that Reilly was murdered. While suicide is possible, it's not probable."

"I'd say the odds of him killing himself are slim to none," said Zak with his usual confidence. "We've had remarkable success in reconstructing what happened. The funeral director took photos of the body when it arrived, and they proved to be very helpful."

I looked at Gus. "I have a little trouble imagining Jason Grubbs as helpful."

"I suggested that an IRS audit of his business might disallow some of his travel deduction claims," said Gus. "Everyone claims things that would be disallowed in an audit. Apparently, Mr. Grubbs decided being helpful was better than paying a tax attorney."

Zak handed me a folder with Reilly's name on it, but I didn't open it. "The pictures show the wound just where we found it. But they also show scratches on his chest. There were blood trails on his shirt confirming that the scratches were premortem. Something scratched him just before he was shot."

Again, he questioned me with his eyes. "A cat," I said. "He had a cat on his lap."

"Exactly."

"What does that mean?" I asked.

Zak gave me a puzzled look. "It doesn't mean anything. I'm just trying to create an accurate picture of the moments before Mr. Heartwood died."

Zak hooked a piece of string to the end of the rod protruding from the dummy's chest, stepped over the coffee table, then fastened the other end to a vertical rod mounted on a tripod. "Bullets travel in straight lines until they hit something," he said, and began raising the rod while looking at a display on the side of the tripod. "The string represents the height of the gun at the moment it was fired. We know the shooter wasn't shooting point-blank because the barrel flash did not burn Reilly's clothes. Your friend Jason kept Reilly's clothing in its natural state. I found a spray of cordite and packing material that put the distance at no less than three feet and no more than seven feet."

He motioned for me to stand in front of the coffee table, handed me a gun, then stepped behind me. "If the gun were fired from here and you were the shooter, you would have to hold it about here."

As positioned by Zak, the only way I could align myself with the string was to hold the gun down by my thigh. "It doesn't seem like a natural shot," I said.

"Right," said Zak. "So either you're standing in the wrong place or you're too tall. Now step over the coffee table. To shoot from in front of the table, the most likely shot, you'd have to be about five-four. To be within our seven foot limit, you could be no more than six-five."

"That's two-thirds of the population," I said, not hiding my annoyance.

"As I said, it depends on where the shooter is standing."

I imagined Tom arguing with Reilly, demanding that Reilly sell the poor farm. Reilly's temper kicks in like lightning, startling the cat. A moment later, Tom shoots Reilly, maybe unintentionally, maybe because testosterone in large amounts is lethal to reason. I imagined it, but I kept seeing the pain in Tom's eyes as he spoke about Amy. I tried to imagine Darrel Potter in the same scene, but he'd have to be about four feet away for the bullet to follow the path established by the string. Darrel was bitter, but I didn't know if he could shoot Reilly while looking him in the eye.

"I thought you had an answer for everything," I said.

"We know a lot considering what we had to work with," said Gus. "It's all in the folder. Photographs, trajectory analyses, and notes. None of this evidence can be used in court. Even if a lawyer managed to get it admitted, we've got nothing that would convict anyone."

"So we know Reilly was murdered, but we don't know who did it?" I had asked a question that didn't require an answer. I turned and looked at the dummy sitting where Reilly had taken his last breath. I knew for certain that someone shot him. The same person killed Jeb and nearly killed me. Reilly and Jeb were connected as attorney and client. Maybe it was the poor farm deal, or maybe it was the guys from Tennessee that Deputy Tittle talked about. If what Tom had told me was true, he seemed an unlikely suspect. I could see Darrel killing Reilly, but not killing Jeb, which meant that if I promoted Darrel to my leading suspect list, I'd have to accept the fact that Jeb's murder and my beating were unrelated.

I let my mind engage these thoughts until I couldn't deal with them any more. The essence of my suspicions was my own guilt, my own need to find an explanation for Reilly's death. Maybe I even wanted retribution. The likelihood was that neither of these men killed anyone. Maybe I needed to recognize that no one was going to be prosecuted for killing either Reilly or Jeb.

I walked Gus and Zak to the front door. "You're going to have to live with this," said Gus. "Don't do anything stupid. You won't get away with it."

I assured him that I wouldn't unilaterally convict someone for murder, then carry out the sentence.

I watched Gus and Zak walk to the end of the driveway. I had learned a lot, but not enough. And I had no idea what I was going to do. LJ appeared with the cordless phone. "Some lady wants to talk to you."

I thought it might by Cali, but the voice belonged to Amy. "I just heard what happened to you. Are you okay?"

I assured her I was, but that I was tired. She didn't take the hint. "I know Tom talked to you. I'm sorry to get you involved in our dirty laundry. I suspect he told you that I have a drug problem, then played the loving husband shtick. He did the same in front of our marriage counselor. You need to be careful. He'll do anything to get his way."

"I really . . ."

"You know he hit Reilly."

For a moment, I was stunned. "What do you mean?"

"I thought the sheriff had told you. Deputy Tittle had to come and break it up. That was last week. Tom threatened him. Reilly said something back and Tom hit him. You can ask Deputy Tittle."

Before I could respond, her interest in talking ended. "I have to go," she said, and hung up.

I found myself caught between husband and wife, each one trying to convince me that the other was a bottom feeder. I'd already decided that the Stewarts were made for each other. For reasons of her own, Amy wanted me to accuse Tom of murdering Reilly. I wasn't interested in playing her game. I doubted what she said was true. If Tom had decked Reilly, it didn't prove anything. Even so, Amy's latest accusation was easily checked, and I needed to get out of the house.

My car had been taken from outside Jeb's office, inspected by the police, and left with Sheriff Belamy. I wasn't supposed to drive for a few days anyway, the thought being that since I might still drop dead any time, having me on the road was not the best idea. Over Frieda's objections, I asked Lora Jean to assist me in adjusting a sling for my right arm, then helped me into my parka. I was going to talk to the sheriff.

The spring-like weather had given way to a cold wind and a threatening sky. Yesterday, it had been near seventy degrees. Today, two days before Christmas, there was talk of snow.

I walked out the front gate and down the hill to town. People were walking slowly past me, waiting their turn to view the remains of C.C. Hollinger. Others were exiting the house, some weeping. The contrast between his fans who genuinely seemed to miss him, and the town, which didn't seem to care he was dead, was overpowering.

The line of mourners already stretched as far as I could see. State troopers were managing the crowd and conversing with the visitors about how long it would take for everyone to get inside, and about how much they liked C.C. Hollinger's "White Lightning" album. To someone's credit, the street had been blocked off to vehicular traffic, and porta-potties had been set up along the side of the road.

I found the sheriff's office, but no one was there. Although it hadn't occurred to me before I left the house, the sheriff and his deputy were most likely helping with crowd control.

Rather than return to the house, I decided to head to the church, where I could ask the Reverend Billy about Reilly's funeral. As the church came into view, I heard Cali's voice call out to me.

"I've been looking for you," she said breathlessly. "Where have you been?"

"Looking for love," I said.

"I hope you did better today than last night." She took my hand. "I want you to come with me. I want you to meet some-one."

"Who?"

"A woman who knew Reilly. A woman who may be able to tell you what made C.C. Hollinger tick."

Chapter 18

Cali reminded me of her visit to the church where Courtney Hollinger was buried, about Sam Jones, the church minister, and Mattie Devereaux, the original minister's sister. All of this was vaguely familiar to me, like someone describing a television show I had dozed through.

When I asked how the Reverend Jones knew Reilly, Cali got exasperated. "I'll go through this again, but I expect you to listen," she said. "The Reverend Jones is the current minister of the church where Courtney is buried. Jones doesn't know Reilly, but the original minister and Reilly were good friends. The Reverend Jones does know Mattie Devereaux, who is the original minister's sister. Mattie has letters written by C.C. Hollinger to her brother. We are going to ask her about the letters and if she knows anything about Courtney Hollinger. Clear?"

"Got it," I said.

"I hope so," said Cali. "I asked Reverend Jones to see if we could visit Mattie. He mentioned you, and Mattie recognized your name. Mattie isn't keen on having visitors, so he's going to meet us at her house. So we are clear on who we are meeting and why?"

"As a bell," I said.

"Now tell me what you've been up to," she replied.

"You are very business-like this morning," I offered.

"Thank you," she said curtly.

Cali listened intently as I described my latest discussion with Gus and Zak. The thought crossed my mind that she'd forgotten all about writing my story. Reilly's professional life as C.C. Hollinger and his unsolved murder were far more compelling than "going-to-jail" tragedies, which are a dime a dozen. Reilly's was the story of a man who walked away from his home and changed his name, a man who was hated by the town he grew up in and returned to, of a star adored by his fans, of someone somehow connected to the death of an innocent man denied justice. Reilly's was a one-of-a-kind story, full of contradictions and half-truths begging for resolution.

We pulled in front of a small clapboard cottage in a neighborhood of similar houses. Mattie's house was freshly painted. Christmas decorations were visible, but tastefully subtle. A fresh pine wreath hung from the door, and inside each window was a red or green candle.

The Reverend Jones was a handsome, youngish man, but with a gray tinge to his sideburns. He smiled at me and shook my left hand. "I heard what happened to you," he said, "and I prayed for you."

"Well, it must have helped," I said.

He looked at the house, then at us. "Mattie is a very sweet lady, but she can have an attitude." He took a breath. "I don't know what she might say, but you can't take it personal. She's seen a lot of cruelty in her life and sometimes she isn't careful who she holds accountable."

The door opened before we had a chance to knock. Mattie gave the Reverend a disapproving glance. She did not look at

Cali or me, but walked into the living room and took a seat in an easy chair. Her eyes ignored us as we walked in to join her.

Mattie was a large woman, but not fat. Her age was indeterminate, although she was clearly old. She wore a wig of gray hair that was slightly crooked and needed combing.

"I don't know what Preacher Jones has told you," said Mattie, "but I'm not much on talking with strangers. Two young whites show up at my door and they gotta be liberals or trying to sell me something. I don't have much time for either, especially liberals. A church burns down and they come out of the woodwork to help the poor black folk build a new church. I hopes it makes 'em feel better, 'cause it doesn't do anything for me. I think they do it 'cause they're afraid that all the coloreds might show up at their churches one Sunday morning and teach the youngsters what praising the Lord is really all about."

"Mattie," said the Reverend Jones. "Mr. Harrington is here to ask about Reilly Heartwood, the man you know as C.C. Hollinger."

"I know that," she snapped. "He's the man that got whacked in the head the other night. Saw that on TV." Mattie glanced at Cali. "So what's *she* doing here?"

"Cali drove me," I said. "On account of me getting whacked in the head."

Mattie looked at me for the first time. I saw a smile at the corners of her mouth, but she did her best to hide it.

"Maybe they didn't hit you hard enough."

I liked her. "I don't want to waste your time," I said, "so I'll get right to the point. Do you know why Reilly took the name Hollinger?"

"Not a big secret, at least not to Courtney's friends." She slid her upper plate out, then clicked it back into place.

"Courtney was working the county fair. In those days, it was legal for black folk to go, but not smart. Courtney was tending the pony ride most of the morning. About mid-day under an oak tree, he took his lunch. He washed it down with some shine and sat down to take a nap. This woman, Rose something, and a man named Randy. ..."

"Rose Abernathy?"

"Yes sir. Rose Abernathy. Rose comes by with Randy, who's smooching her, but she's not letting on whether she likes him or not. Drives a man crazy not knowing whether he's going to get what he wants." She looked at Cali. "You should never tease a man 'cause he's got no control when his blood gets hot."

She clicked her teeth for a moment. "Rose takes Courtney's jug and takes a drink. Randy takes a drink and then tries to have his way with Rose. But Rose's brother shows up and punches Randy, who falls and hits his head on a rock. Courtney jumps up and Rose gets to screaming. When everyone arrives, he's leaning over Randy. Everyone thinks he did it because he's black. But Reilly Heartwood knew it weren't true. I know that 'cause I heard him talking to my brother, the good Reverend James Andrews, God rest his soul. Reilly carried a heavy load for his staying quiet and Courtney being killed in jail. He and James talked a lot."

I was stunned and speechless.

"But why didn't Reilly come forward?" asked Cali.

"I never said I'd answer a hundred questions. I'm just telling you a story. I remember Mr. Heartwood trying to do his best to take care of the Hollingers after Courtney was killed, but all the money in the world wasn't going to make it right or make his heart ache any less."

We sat for a moment in silence. Then Mattie looked at me and said, "You know, you sound like him."

"Excuse me?"

"Mr. Heartwood. Your daddy. You sound like him."

The room fell silent. Cali's mouth was as wide open as mine. The Reverend Jones was on the edge of his chair. Mattie's eyes fixed on mine. "Well, I guess I've let the cat out of the bag," she said with a deep laugh. "Great God and Caesar's ghost, you didn't know. If that don't beat all."

She picked up a shoebox and shuffled over to me. "These letters are mostly about you. How he missed you. How you were growing up tall and strong. The man adored you."

I took the box, but I still couldn't manage to say anything. I tried to wrap my head around the idea that the man who had been like a father to me *was* my father. I was bombarded with emotions, none of which stuck, and all of which left me bewildered. I had the answer to one question about Reilly, only to have it lead to a hundred more.

"I read them letters when my brother died," said Mattie. "I know it wasn't right, but Reilly being famous and all...." She shook her head. "I couldn't resist. I read one and then another. I didn't mean any harm."

I touched the letters, wondering what other secrets they would expose. Finally I managed to speak. "What happened between Reilly and my mother? Why did my mother marry Russell Harrington?"

Mattie patted my hand. She sighed, then picked a letter out of the box. "This letter I read a lot 'cause it tells what happened to Reilly and your momma." I felt her hand touch my cheek. "Grief don't care about the color of your skin. If it helps some, Mr. Heartwood didn't know that you were his until a long time after you were born. He thought your mamma had gotten in with this Harrington fellow. The fact is, your real daddy never loved anyone 'cept your mother, and she loved him. Somewhere, that truth got lost and the two of them separated. It's a tragedy, like what happened to Courtney."

I stood up slowly, and looked down at Mattie Devereaux. I saw sadness in her face. She was no stranger to tragedy or the pain that human foolishness can cause. She took no pleasure in mine. "Thank you," I said.

I was a victim of this real-life melodrama, but only incidentally so. I now had a context for the loneliness and bitterness I had seen in my mother. I remembered seeing her crying when she thought she was alone, when her stoic facade failed her and she indulged a moment of self-pity. Whatever the truth meant to me personally, whatever emotion I chose to wallow in, I couldn't claim that I'd been cheated out of the things that matter. William Harrington, the man who gave me his name, who loved me from a distance, couldn't compete with the pathos of lost love between Reilly and my mother. This was a tragedy owned by three people. I was merely an observer and, by relative standards, an incidental victim. But victim or not, I'd been cheated out of my time with Reilly and was determined to find out by whom.

When I turned to Cali, she was wiping her eyes. The Reverend Jones was similarly touched. I took the letters and thanked Mattie again, then walked to the door.

When we got to Cali's car, I told her I wanted to pick up my car at the sheriff's office and drive it back to Reilly's house. She seemed to sense something wasn't right. I answered every question, refused to sulk, and painted every event in an objective light. I was, by all outward measures, calm. I suspect that's what made her suspicious. She kept probing, but I was steadfastly rational.

After a time, Cali focused on her driving. I read the letter that Mattie had selected several times, then put it away and stared out the window.

We left the interstate and took a two-lane highway that cut through the rolling countryside. Some distance from the road, I saw an old, abandoned farmhouse, its weathered exterior silvered by years of neglect. I imagined children playing on the porch, their voices squealing with the joy of the moment. I wondered if they'd left this house for a better opportunity somewhere else, or if some tragedy had beset them, ripping them from their house and stifling their dreams. As the house disappeared from view, I felt bad for the imaginary family even as I envied them.

Most of the traffic was heading away from Lyle. Fans had made their trek and offered their respects to Reilly. They had come to thank a man whose music brought them so much pleasure, but none of them knew that his music was born from a tragic decision he'd made when he was just twenty-seven. I watched the long line of cars with an odd mixture of pride and sadness.

When we got close to the center of town, the street was still jammed with cars and people. Cali pulled into a parking spot a block from Main Street. I thanked her, hoping she'd leave, but she took the keys from the ignition. "I don't know you well enough to be worried about you, but I am anyway." She slid out of the car and joined me on the sidewalk.

As we approached the sheriff's office, Cali took hold of my arm. "Reilly's death has turned into a media circus," she said. "I know some of these people, and they don't get out in the street for nothing."

We pushed our way through the throng, then stepped over a sawhorse intended to keep the doorway clear. The crowd, forced into the street, was blocking traffic. Deputy Lou Tittle was yelling at a satellite truck driver and didn't notice us until we reached the door.

"Where in hell do you think you're going?" he yelled, hitching up his pants. He was speaking to me, but his eyes were on Cali, scanning her from the hips upward.

"To get my car."

"You crossed an official police line, asshole," he said.

"Arrest me, take me inside, and give me my car," I said.

As I opened the door and stepped inside, I met the unhappy face of Sheriff Belamy.

"What's happening?" I asked.

"An hour ago, Darrel Potter confessed to killing Reilly," replied Belamy.

Doc was there, glaring at me. "You couldn't leave it alone? You had to know? Well then, now you do."

"Just a God damned minute," I said. "A man was murdered. Doesn't that matter to you?"

"What matters to me," said Doc, "is that Darrel Potter is going to die in prison because you couldn't leave things the way they were. Reilly was dead. What did it matter how he got that way? He isn't coming back."

I couldn't fathom why Doc was so concerned about Darrel. But even as I tried, I was getting the feeling that Darrel's confession was bullshit.

"I'll need to have a word with Darrel Potter," I said, stepping toward the counter that divided the room.

Deputy Tittle grabbed my arm. I was in no mood to be grabbed. In a single move, I broke his grip, took hold of his wrist, and pushed him into the wall. He rolled to the floor, and came to his knees with his gun in both hands. I heard the hammer cock.

"You better shoot straight, Tittle," I said, "before I rip your throat out."

"Put it down!" screamed the sheriff. "And you," he said looking at me, "you back off. I've had enough of you."

"Let me see Darrel," I said, "and then I'll leave."

The sheriff glared at me. "You've got no business seeing anyone."

"I think I have a right to talk to the man who killed my father," I replied.

The silence was deafening. I looked at Doc. "Did you know that Reilly was my father?"

He answered with an expression of shock and sorrow. "No. I didn't know." He looked like he was about to say more, then shook his head and went outside.

The sheriff sighed. "I can't let you talk to him," he said softly. "Maybe later, with his attorney present."

Cali tugged at my arm. "Let's go, Shep," she said.

Pain now shot through my ribs, head, and arm. I headed to the door, then answered, "I'll be around until someone tells me the truth."

Chapter 19

Over Cali's objections, I drove my car back to Reilly's house. As we pulled in the driveway, I saw a man putting red carpet into the back of a truck. I was hunched over, holding my side, rocking unsteadily as I approached the man. I must have looked drunk because at first he gave me a disapproving look. As I got closer, he seemed to recognize me. He handed me a key and said, "I was told to lock up if you didn't get back before I left."

I thanked him and we went inside. Cali offered to help me upstairs, but I headed for the living room. Despite a fire in the fireplace, the house was cold from the viewing. She stayed back as I approached the casket. I touched Reilly's cheek, then closed the lid.

"I'm very sorry about dragging you into this insanity," I said to her. "You've been very kind, and I appreciate everything you've done."

"It sounds like you're quitting."

"I'm not quitting. But I don't want you involved in this. The next time someone decides to beat the crap out of me, I don't want you around."

"But Darrel confessed to killing Reilly."

"Right," I said. "And maybe Santa was his accomplice."

"You don't think he did it?"

"I don't want you involved," I said, avoiding her question.

"Let's get something straight," Cali shot back. "You and your family and this town may be absolutely mad, but I'm hooked. I want to find out how all this ends. Call it Pulitzer envy, but I smell a story that might just get me out of this place. So that's where I'm coming from."

I walked over to a chair and sat in front of the fire. Cali was right, but the events of the day had taken everything out of me. "Darrel Potter says he killed Reilly," I said. "He was one of my suspects. Of course, to have shot him in cold blood with one bullet to the heart, he'd have to have stood about four feet from Reilly. Darrel can hardly hold a cigarette, much less a gun." A thought crossed my mind, more like a feeling that I'd said something that mattered. But the thought vanished, and I was unable to reconstruct it. "So why would he confess? I mean, even if he did it, why confess now?"

Cali kneeled in front of me. "Exactly. Let me see the report Gus gave you."

I went to my room. When I returned, Cali offered me a plate of leftovers, a glass of water, and a bottle of aspirin. She read the report while I sat in front of the fire, sorting through events and trying to make decisions. With the help of a large portion of meatloaf and potatoes and a double dose of aspirin, my aches and pains became tolerable.

I looked at Cali and caught her gazing into the fire.

"You want to talk about it?" I asked.

"About what?"

"You had that sad look again. Sometimes talking about an old hurt makes it better. Sometimes it doesn't. I was just offering to listen."

"The sad look?" she said shaking her head. "I've been working for the paper for over a year and no one said anything about my sad look." I heard her sigh as she averted her eyes. "How can you have time to listen to me after all you've been through?"

"I'm in between revelations right now. I guess I'm just bored."

A smile flickered on her face, but didn't stay. "Not much of a story. I had the perfect life with the perfect man in the perfect house. We both had decent jobs. I didn't think about the future because I was so happy. One night I got upset because we were out of milk. I badgered Drew, my husband, into running a quick errand so we'd have milk for cereal in the morning. He was tired, but I pushed him."

Tears trickled down Cali's cheeks and she wiped them away with a trembling hand. "On his way back from the supermarket, a drunk driver hit him head on. The last words I said to the man I adored was to be certain to get two-percent." She looked at me. "You remind me of him in some ways. In other ways, you remind me of me. Only you're more together."

"You mean putting aside my desire to kill Tom Stewart and Darrel Potter? You know, just to be sure?"

"No. Because, despite all that's happened to you, you're not bitter. You're crazy, but you're not blaming the world for what's happened to you. I don't understand how you do that." She wiped her eyes on her sleeve. "I'm going to freshen up."

Cali returned and studied the files. I let her be, busying myself with trying to figure out what it was about Darrel's confession that bothered me. Why couldn't I be content to accept it?

I chewed on the confession awhile, then turned my thoughts to Reilly's funeral. I wasn't any more successful with that line of inquiry, finding myself stuck on why I should apologize to Rose and how I would explain it to Sarah if I did.

Cali cleared her throat. "Can I ask you a question?"

"You just did."

"Why is it when men feel better, they act like assholes?"

"It's our way of sending a signal. If I said anything else, I'd be sulking."

Cali nodded. "Very good. You might just be trainable."

"So the question is...?"

"Let's assume Darrel Potter didn't kill Reilly. So why would he say he did? He wouldn't protect Tom. But he might protect someone else. And you say Doc has been defensive about things. Who would he protect?"

I considered how obvious the observation was, then said, "Rodney, his grandson."

It occurred to me that if Doc was going to compromise his standards, it might be for a teenager whose life was still in front of him. But as I imagined Rodney standing in front of Reilly pointing a gun at him, I got another odd feeling. Something was wrong with that picture as well, but I couldn't put my finger on it.

"You're making a face," said Cali.

"Sorry. Something popped into my head. Read me the section of the police report about how Doc reported the shooting."

"All it says is that he called at 7:45. Why?"

"Let me see the file." I looked over the report, then flipped to the death certificate. And that's when it hit me.

"What are you smiling about?"

"Doc reported the time of death as 7:15 P.M. What happened during those thirty minutes?"

"This doesn't make any sense," said Cali, stating aloud what I was thinking.

"And we can waste a lot of time trying to unravel the riddle."

"You have other plans?"

"Yes we do," I said, carefully extricating myself from my chair.

With the setting of the sun, Lyle became a ghost town. Everyone in Lyle was where he or she wanted to be, which was either at Mac's Bar, the bowling alley, or home.

The Reverend Billy lived in a small cottage behind the church. I rang the doorbell and we waited. The screen door creaked and the wind rattled leaves, but no sound came from inside. Expectation faded into doubt. Finally, I concluded that no one was home. I peered in the windows that fronted the porch, past the light fabric of the curtains. On the floor were the trappings of someone just moving in, or getting ready to move out. Boxes were scattered about and things piled nearby.

I led Cali back to the church and went inside. The front door slammed behind us, filling the empty chapel with a thunderous rumble. Though the rectory door was closed, I could hear the dull boom of Billy's voice exhorting God to explain something. There was a moment of silence followed by another muffled demand. It had the cadence of a conversation, and I wondered if Billy was alone. I opened the door slowly as Billy's voice again exploded.

"If You are what we think, why haven't You helped me?!

Why is it when You are needed most, You seem to leave us to dangle? Do You enjoy our suffering?"

Billy stared at me, then staggered backward. "I'm having a private discussion with my Lord, if you don't mind," he said, his words slurred.

"We need to talk," I demanded.

"You can talk to God anywhere you want," responded Billy, "except here."

Billy stared past me, then said, "I heard that you and Rose haven't exactly reached an accord on what to do about Reilly."

"For Christ's sake, Billy. My mother was your friend. Reilly was your friend. I thought I was your friend. You know how Rose treated my mother and yet you want me to apologize? What kind of a friend is that?"

Billy drained his glass. "The person with the problem isn't you or your mother. It's Reilly," responded Billy in his preacher's voice. He belched, then grabbed hold of the corner of the desk to keep from falling. "I loved your mother," he added somberly.

"All you have to do is bury the man," I said. "Is that too much to ask?"

"More than you know," replied Billy weakly.

"What's so difficult about digging a hole and putting the man's body in it?" The color drained from Billy's face and his eyes glazed over. "Billy?" I said, pleading. "What are you so afraid of?"

"I've always been afraid of something," said Billy. He looked at me and tried to speak. As his eyes rolled back in his head and he fell over, I ran to him. Even in my best condition, I wouldn't have been able to break his fall. He hit the floor with an ominous grunt, then rolled over on his back.

Cali knelt beside him, then placed two fingers on his neck. "His pulse is strong," she said. "I think he just passed out."

I moved Billy so that he was lying flat, then called Doc. Following Doc's directions, I placed a cushion under Billy's feet. I took comfort in Doc's insistence that there was nothing to worry about, that this had happened to Billy before. Even so, I looked with consternation upon the pale stillness that had taken over Billy's unconscious form.

Ten minutes later, I heard the echo of the door to the church as it slammed shut. Doc appeared and Billy became *his* problem.

Doc nodded at me, then at Cali. He slowly lowered himself so he could kneel beside Billy. Doc mumbled, said "yes" a few times, nodded again, then stood up. "He's sleeping. Valium and whiskey. Quite a sedative. He'll sleep it off." Doc looked at me as if he were going to say more, waved his hand, then shuffled his way to the door.

"I talked to Terry," I said. "He told me why Rose wants me to apologize."

Doc paused at the door to the rectory, his knees slightly bent to make up for the weakness in his hips. "I heard."

"I had a right to know," I said, "about how mom cleaned floors for the Abernathys."

Doc marched over to me and stuck a bony finger in my chest. "Your mother owned her past, not you. You got no right to know squat about it unless she decided to share it with you."

I felt the hair on my arms stand up. "So you think I should apologize to Rose after all the suffering Rose and her family caused my mother and grandmother? Is that your solution to Reilly's dilemma?"

Doc closed his eyes and shook his head. "So righteous are the young—and so stupid." His face softened. "Mary has willed you a very large banana, and you have clutched it like it was something precious. Just like a monkey." Doc lowered himself into a pew. "Sit, monkey."

"Doc," I said softly, "I think I've missed something."

"Course you have. To catch a monkey, you take a box and cut a hole in it just big enough for the monkey's hand. Inside the box you put a banana. Monkeys love bananas more than anything. So when the monkey grabs the banana, he's ecstatic. But the banana won't fit through the hole. Even if a lion, or a tiger, or men with nets come toward the monkey, he won't let go, even though letting go would save him."

"I think I saw this on cable," I said. "One of the National Geographic specials."

"You can be as dense as stone. It's not television we're discussing but life. People treat the inequities of life like bananas. They hold on to them even though letting go would make them much happier. Your mother held her grudge against Rose well after it ceased to make any sense. Now *you* have it. Reilly lies in need of a funeral. But pride, *your* pride, denies him his final resting place."

"You're saying it's my fault?"

Doc closed his eyes again. "Blame is such a terrible thing to waste. No, it's not your fault. It's your choice, son. People like Rose don't make life miserable for good people. They make good people choose. Reilly chose to leave town, leaving the good folk of Lyle penniless. Reilly didn't make them that way. But Reilly's fame gave them a choice. They chose to gamble their futures on events they couldn't control. They can't accept the consequences of their own decisions, so they blame Reilly. Worse, they pass down their misdirected hatred to their kids. There are people in this town who never met Reilly but thought he was a cheat."

"I'm sorry," I said, "I still don't get what you're saying."

"Rose has offered you a choice," Doc said. "You can bury Reilly by choosing to apologize. I'm not saying it's an easy decision. But it is one you can make."

I looked to Cali. I could see that she agreed with Doc. I didn't bring her along to be outnumbered. She sensed my dismay and shrugged. I wasn't giving up the banana just yet.

"But why won't Billy just stand up to Rose?"

Doc rubbed his eyes. "Billy spent years hiding under his bed, hoping to avoid a beating from his father. He hated school because the kids taunted him for being fat. One day, he broke the nose of a kid who called him a name. The kid's father pressed charges, and Billy was put in a jail cell with men twice his age. The inmates touched him, and he fought back. He slammed one of them into the bars of his cell and killed him. He was convicted of manslaughter and sent to prison.

"On his way to a halfway house, he was accidentally put on the wrong bus. He ended up here. We thought he was the new preacher, and that's what he became. Rose, Reilly, your mother and I are the only ones who know. Rose has threatened to expose him. So, if you force Billy to bury Reilly and you don't apologize, Rose exposes Billy, and he goes back to prison to complete his sentence. Again, it's your choice."

I rubbed my temples. My head was processing what Doc had said while working on something else just out of the range of my perception. The image of Rodney came to me again, this time more focused. He sees his mother hit by his grandfather, all the while knowing that the source of his grandfather's anger is Reilly Heartwood. He's had enough. He takes Darrel's gun and heads off to kill Reilly. The theory seems to fit the facts, but not perfectly enough to make me buy it.

I looked at Doc and then at Cali. "Tell Billy to arrange things for tomorrow, that I'll make Rose happy."

Doc sighed. "Thank you," he said, starting to get up.

"One more question. Actually, a hypothetical. Let's say there's this kid whose grandfather is beating the kid's mother. The kid blames this rich guy for all his troubles and goes to the rich guy's house and shoots him."

"I don't have time for this," said Doc.

"But a friend of the family comes to the scene and decides that allowing a kid to go to prison for the rest of his life is a greater tragedy than the murder of a rich, aging singer who lots of folks despise. So the friend helps the kid by making it look like the rich guy shot himself."

Doc got to his feet, but I grabbed his hand. "But what if the kid didn't do it. What if the kid and the friend only thought the kid was the shooter? Wouldn't it be better for the kid not to go through life thinking he shot a man in cold blood?"

Doc eyed me. "If that were the case, hypothetically, I'd agree that it would be better for the boy."

"Let's say I wanted to talk to this boy right away and agreed not to tell or do anything unless I could prove he didn't shoot anyone. Could that be arranged?"

"I wouldn't know," said Doc.

"Thanks." As Doc left, I said, "I guess sometimes you can be holding a banana and not even know it."

He glanced at me over his shoulder. I could see some doubt in Doc's face. Then he was gone.

"What was that all about?" asked Cali.

"I'm working on a new theory," I said.

"It doesn't involve killing anyone, does it?"

"I hope not."

Chapter 20

The Potter house was across town, meaning it took all of five minutes to get there. I wasn't sure what would happen if Rodney answered the door. I rapped on the door with a heavy brass doorknocker and waited.

A woman came to the door. It took me a moment to realize that she was Carla Tierney, Rodney's mother. Given Rodney's age, I figured she was, at most, forty-two or three, but the face that looked back at me strongly suggested she was old well beyond her years. A dark welt on her left cheek confirmed Darrel's alibi.

"Who are you?" she demanded, a mixture of annoyance and fear in her voice.

"I'm Shep Harrington." She nodded, so I knew Doc had called. "Is Rodney here?"

"He's in his room. He won't come out."

"I don't think he killed Reilly, Mrs. Tierney."

She swung the door open and glowered at me. "Haven't you caused enough trouble? Reilly ruined my father's life. Now you've ruined my son's and mine. What's with you people?"

I ignored her. "Did Darrel keep his gun loaded?"

The question distracted her. "Yes. I don't like guns, but he was afraid of some men he used to hang out with. He would load and unload that gun all night."

I sighed. "If Rodney will come with me, I think we can fix this in short order. If I'm wrong, I'll leave town and say no more about it."

"Rodney said the gun went off by accident. He didn't mean to shoot him." She was sobbing, her body shaking. "Dad is a lot of bad things, but he doesn't want Rodney to spend his life in prison."

"If I'm correct about what happened the night Reilly was killed, neither of them will be going to prison. But I need your help."

"You want *my* help? After all the trouble you've caused? You can go to hell, Mr. Harrington."

She tried to close the door, but I blocked it with my foot. "To be honest with you, Mrs. Tierney, I'm too tired to convince you to do anything. But you stay home tonight and your father could die in prison. Your son will have to cope with the guilt of killing a man and letting your father take the blame. You should trust me because you've got nothing to lose and everything to gain."

She looked intently at me for a moment, then slammed the door in my face.

Cali was waiting for me in the car. "What did she say?"

"She said we're missing a bullet."

Cali and I were in Reilly's study with Doc when Carla Tierney arrived with her son, Rodney. Rodney looked frail, like a tree that had grown too fast. Take away the sullen arrogance of youth, and what remained was a scared boy. Even so, he towered over every one in the room but me. He was easily six-three, about Tom's height.

Most males kill something when they are growing up: a bird, a rabbit, or some other small creature. The event usually stirs the conscience. The animal is sacrificed to teach the world's most dangerous predator a lesson in mortality. Some learn it. Some don't. Rodney was now taking the lesson to its limit. In his own mind, he had killed a man. His puffy, watery eyes revealed that it had not set well with him.

"We're going to reenact the night Reilly died," I said. I offered Rodney a gun.

"Where did that come from?" demanded Doc.

"You don't always make friends in prison," I said without apology. He seemed unconvinced. "After getting out of prison, I received death threats from people in my old company who thought I should have stayed in prison until their stock options vested. I've been shot at three times. Any more questions?"

Rodney looked at the weapon like it would bite. "I don't want to do this."

"You didn't kill him," I said.

"I did. I shot him. Gramps didn't do it. I didn't mean to, but...."

I looked at Carla. "Do what he says," she said softly.

Rodney wiped his eyes and took the gun.

I said to Rodney. "Think back. When you came in the room, what did you see?"

He rolled his eyes. "I saw Mr. Heartwood on the couch."

"Was there a cat in his lap?"

Rodney nodded. "A big black one."

"The marks on Reilly's chest," said Doc out loud.

I walked Rodney over to the couch and told him to stand

where he was the night Reilly died.

He stood just in front of the coffee table. I could see immediately from the string Zak had used to mark the bullet's path that Rodney was too tall to have fired the fatal shot. "So you were about four feet away?"

"Yeah."

"Do and say what you did that night."

Rodney raised the gun and pointed it at the dummy. I imagined Reilly facing the barrel of a gun held by an angry, nervous teenager. "I told him he had ruined Gramps' life and my mom's life. I told him that it was his fault that Gramps beat Mom. I told him I hated him."

I heard Carla stifle a sob.

"What did he say?"

"He said he understood why I thought that, but it wasn't true. He had tried to help Gramps. I told him he was lying, but I knew he wasn't."

"Did you shoot him then?"

Rodney shook his head. "I stared at him for a long time. All I could hear was my heart pounding in my head. Then I heard a noise and the gun went off and Reilly died."

Rodney threw the gun down and ran to the door. I grabbed him, but he pushed me away. "Fuck you."

"You want to rot in prison for something you didn't do? Go ahead. Make your mother miserable for the rest of her life. Or stop acting like an idiot and finish this."

If at that moment Rodney had a real gun, I'm certain he would have shot me.

Doc stepped between us. "Remember, Shep, that if you're

wrong about this, you don't say anything to anyone."

I nodded and Rodney picked up the gun and stood in front of Reilly's surrogate. "You heard a noise. Did you turn your head?"

"Yeah. I looked over toward the corner by the window. The gun went off and Reilly grabbed his chest."

"Point the gun at the dummy and put your finger on the trigger," I said.

"Are you going to get to the point?" demanded Carla.

I stepped behind Rodney. "You're looking at the man who made your grandfather a mean drunk who beats your mother. You're thinking bad thoughts. You're angry. Like you're angry with me now. Now turn toward the window and pull the trigger. Don't worry. The gun's not loaded."

As Rodney turned, the barrel of the gun rose sharply. The click of the firing pin was as loud as the crack of gunfire. I grabbed his hand and held it in place. "You didn't shoot Reilly. Your shot hit the wall just behind the Christmas tree."

"The empty chamber," said Cali. "One casing, one empty chamber. Two bullets. Two shooters. With Reilly's broken foot, he was stuck on the couch. The second shooter merely came along, picked up the gun, and shot him."

"The gunshot scared the cat, who dug his rear claws into Reilly's chest. Reilly grabbed his chest, making it look like he was hit."

"Then who killed Reilly?" asked Carla.

I shook my head. "Someone smart enough to take the extra casing. My guess is we'll never know."

Rodney trembled, then fell to his knees. Carla ran sobbing

to him. While Doc and Cali comforted them, I made my way to the bathroom. The bruises from last night's beating were throbbing in unison and I was suddenly sick to my stomach. I curled up on the floor next to the toilet and lost dinner. I've been sick before, but never with cracked ribs. It's an experience I won't soon forget.

I felt Doc's rough hand on the back of my neck. "When you run on adrenaline, you eventually pay the price. You did a good thing tonight." He handed me a damp washcloth. "I feel like a fool—an old fool at that."

"No need for that, Doc. You were faced with a choice and you chose. Believing what you believed, I can't say it was the wrong choice. But until the truth is known, no decision is risk free."

"Carla called me. Rodney had come home in a panic saying he'd accidentally shot Reilly. When I got here, I found Reilly on the couch. I remember seeing his crutches on the floor. It never occurred to me that Reilly was trying to get off the couch, that he was trying to get away. I just couldn't let Rodney rot in prison, so I arranged everything to make it look like Reilly killed himself." I could see Doc wrestling with his conscience, but I was in no condition to help.

Cali arrived and looked at me. "I think it's time you called it a night."

I got to my knees, then to my feet. I had had a busy day. I'd sprung Darrel from jail and proven that Rodney was not a killer. I had arranged for Reilly to be buried. But I had one more loose end to cover. "Not just yet," I said. "I need to talk to some folks about selling the poor farm."

Chapter 21

Carla, Rodney, and Doc left to talk to the sheriff. Cali made me a cup of tea and stoked the fire. "Are you sure you're up to this? I mean, I don't know what's so important that it can't wait until tomorrow."

"You drive, and I'll try not to hurl," I said.

"As I recall, you promised on our second date you wouldn't lose your lunch. Any more of that and I'll take it personally."

I called Terry and asked if the residents were awake and decent. He assured me that, by the time we arrived, they'd at least be awake.

The residents each have a small apartment that joins a common living room. They were watching a Civil War movie when we arrived. I was about to say something when I was shushed in unison. "This is the good part," said Carrie.

I watched the videotape as a long line of Yankee soldiers paraded past a group of slaves. Cecil leaned back from the couch, and whispered, "We've seen this a hundred times, but each time we find another mistake. In a second, you'll see a young black girl wearing a digital watch."

A moment later, Harry ran to the screen with a remote control. "There!" he yelled, freezing the picture.

Carrie beamed at me. "Everyone makes mistakes," she said.

She turned to Cali. "Hi, sweetie. It's good to see you again."

"Are you and Shep getting married?" asked Cecil.

Before Cali could answer, Jamie handed me a slip of paper. "You're mistaken if you think you're never wrong." I thought back to the Chinese fortune I got at lunch, "Knowing isn't everything." Jamie had a knack for stating what should be obvious.

"Terry said you wanted to talk to us," said Harry, turning off the television.

"I hope it's not bad news," said Carrie. "Most of the time when someone wants to talk, it's bad news."

I could hear Cali stifling a laugh. The residents could be disarming, but they were not to be underestimated. "Let me come right to the point. In his will, Reilly left the farm to me. I have to decide whether to sell the farm or not. People in town and in the county would benefit if the farm were sold. But you all would have to move. I need to know how you feel about living somewhere else."

Four faces stared back at me, but no one answered. A moment passed, then Jamie handed me a note. "Don't tell Reilly."

"Don't tell him what?"

Carrie said, "I think Jamie is saying that Reilly told us not to tell."

"Reilly asked you all the same question?"

"Yes, dear," said Carrie. "He said Doc had urged him to reconsider selling the farm as a way of patching up old wounds. Reilly was worried about us, you see. He was such a dear man."

"And what did you say?"

"He owns the farm now," said Harry. "I guess we can tell

him." Carrie nodded. "Reilly asked if we'd mind living in town in his house. We told him that if we could take our cats with us, we'd move. He said he would talk to his lawyer, then call a meeting with some of the people in town, and it would be done. Then he went and shot himself. Seems like an odd thing to do, don't you think?"

I was getting that feeling again that things weren't adding up.

"Reilly said I could have a room with lots of windows," said Carrie.

"I'll see to it," I said.

Carrie took Cali's hand. "Shep's a good boy. He didn't mean to steal the money."

Apparently the reason for my imprisonment was not clear—I had never been accused of stealing anything.

We were almost to my car when Terry stopped us. "Rose asked me to give you this. It's what she wants you to say in church tomorrow." He looked at his feet. "I know why you're apologizing, but I think it stinks."

I thanked him and crawled into the car. I was getting light-headed and I felt around on the floor for the barf bowl. Cali started the engine, but left the car in park. "I saw the look you gave Harry," said Cali. "Something he said gave you a brain fart, didn't it?"

"A *what?*"

"You were thinking something. What was it?"

"Reilly wanted to have a meeting to tell Chester and the others that he was going to sell the farm to Tom. I've been operating on the assumption that Reilly was killed because he wouldn't sell the farm. So what if somebody killed him because he *was* going to sell it?"

"But no one knew his decision except the residents. I doubt they said anything to anyone."

"Reilly told Jeb," I said out loud, but mostly to myself, "who was going to tell me. Maybe Reilly also told Tom."

"I don't see how that helps," she said. "Tom would be the last one to kill Reilly if he was going to do the deal with Tom's clients."

"Precisely where I'm stuck. There's just something I'm forgetting. I can feel it."

"What you're feeling is exhaustion," said Cali patting my hand.

I took out my wallet and found Tom's card. I dialed the number, reached his answering machine, and left a message that I had a proposition for him and would speak with him after the funeral. Then I called the sheriff and asked him to get me a report of Reilly's phone calls the day he died. The sheriff took a few minutes to thank me and to apologize. I listened politely and finally cut him off.

"What was that all about?" asked Cali.

"Reilly may have called his killer the day he died," I said. "It's a long-shot, but better to cover all the bases."

"You've covered a lot of bases today," she said. "Let it go until tomorrow."

I closed my eyes. As I drifted off to sleep, I was thinking that tomorrow I would bury Reilly and, if my head cleared, also figure out who killed him.

It was going to be a big day.

Chapter 22

Despite my tossing and turning, I managed to sleep until about 6:30, and was out of bed and dressed as the eastern sky brightened. The morning looked cold, and clouds were starting to gather in the west. It was a good day for a funeral.

I fed the cats and checked with Billy. Everything was set for 11:00 a.m. Doc had issued a revised death certificate and Sheriff Belamy had revised his police report. The only thing I had to do now was to get Reilly in the ground.

I walked to the cemetery, then stood just inside the gate. I could see Billy standing by the stone that marked the resting place of my mother's ashes. Nearby was a mound covered by a green carpet. The diggers had come and gone.

Billy arranged some flowers, stepped back, then arranged them again. I made my way up the hill as he knelt down and clasped his hands. I stayed back to give him privacy, but in a moment he was on his feet.

"A friar without a prayer is a naked man indeed," he said turning toward me. "I should stop pretending to be what I've never been."

"That's not fair," I said, draping my arm on his shoulder. "You've been a guiding light around here for years."

"Reilly and your mother knew about me and accepted me

for what I had become, not what I had been. And now you're going to apologize to Rose to save me. You deserve better." Billy touched the gravestone.

I took Billy's hand. "Mom," I said reverently. "I'm going to apologize because Billy's been a good friend and deserves our support. Get over it."

"I'm sorry, Mary," said Billy.

Billy and I walked toward the center of town. Neither of us spoke until we reached the monument to C.C. Hollinger, the one that had started such a ruckus at the town council meeting just a few days before. Someone had tried to clear away the vines and weeds and to polish the stone, but the effort had apparently been too daunting.

"The town didn't deserve him," said Billy. "He helped them when they needed help and took no credit for it. All he wanted was for them to accept him for what he was, not for what they thought he was. He thought if he made them whole, they would understand that the studio mess was caused by a combination of bad luck and bad timing, that they would stop blaming him. He found ways to preserve their dignity by hiding the source of his gifts. But they hated him still."

"Maybe if they'd known," I said, "he'd still be alive."

Billy shrugged. "Or he'd be accused of throwing the poor locals scraps from his table." He shook his head. "I'm sorry, but I'm not feeling very kindly about my fellow man today."

I returned to the house to find Frieda in front of the stove stirring something, staring into space. I stepped between her and the stove. "It's okay, Frieda. It's time to say good-bye. I want you to go into town with Lora Jean and buy the prettiest dresses you can find. I'll take care of the bill. I anticipated her protest and shushed her. "I want you in the first pew of the church and in the lead limo. We are his family and friends and we are going to act like it."

Frieda nodded. As a tear managed to find its way onto her cheek, she turned back to her cooking and busied herself. "Remember," I said, "the prettiest dress you've ever bought."

Frieda laughed. "I don't know if I can still buy a twelve dollar dress."

After breakfast, I called Cali's home number, but she wasn't in. I then called the Eternal Peace Funeral Home and started to work on Jason Grubbs. I listened to a few minutes of Jason's whining, then cut him off. "I'm sorry you were offended," I said.

"Humiliated," countered Jason.

"I'll tell you what," I said finally, "you arrange to have the funeral video-taped, beginning at the funeral home. A couple of shots of your car and of you helping everyone should be good for the funeral directors' show in Las Vegas. What do you say?"

"You'll agree to double the rate because of its being close to Christmas?" I questioned his logic, but agreed. "You're on."

I bought out the florist shops of Lyle and Front Royal, then arranged with Jason to be certain that, after the ceremony, the flowers, save a single wreath, would be divided between the hospital in Front Royal and Reverend Sam Jones's church. Jason commended me on my generosity, offering his assistance for a mere hundred dollars. Dying, I was quickly learning, was an expensive proposition.

I took an exquisitely long shower, then dressed in the best suit I owned. Frieda, Lora Jean, and Sarah were waiting for me in the living room. We chatted about the weather and about Christmas. But when the hearse arrived, the conversation ended. We had reached the beginning of the end, and none of us spoke as Reilly left his house for the last time.

Jason had found a videographer and was offering instructions on how Reilly Heartwood's funeral procession should be captured for posterity. Even so, Sarah, Lora Jean, Frieda, and I had to exit the house three times to be sure the moment was captured to Jason's satisfaction. I had to intervene to make sure Reilly wasn't late for his own service.

The street in front of the small church was packed with people. A sign in front of the door read: "WE REGRET THAT THERE IS NO ROOM INSIDE THE CHURCH."

Jason let the cameraman out of the hearse first, then cued the four of us. Behind us, six tuxedo-clad pallbearers carried the coffin up the stairs of the church. As they stepped inside, the church came alive with whispers, easily heard over the soft moan of an organ. The ladies and I made our way to the front, the whispers turning to shushes as the church, which was standing room only, became still and formal.

We joined Doc, Terry, Terry's wife, and the residents of the poor farm in the front right pew. Rose and some people I didn't know occupied the left pew. I could feel her eyes on me, but I didn't reward her by showing any interest. Reverend Billy appeared at a side door behind the pulpit. He strode to the casket and touched it, then raised his arms. "Forgive us, Reilly, for we know not what friendship is." For a moment, Billy remained by the casket, his eyes fixed on me. Deciding that the time to pay Rose for the right to bury Reilly had arrived, I stood, but Billy motioned for me to be seated.

"For several weeks now," said Billy, his voice slow and serene, "I have been searching for the meaning of Christmas. There were the usual answers—a time of giving, caring, sharing good will. But sometimes we forget the courage of Mary and Joseph and all the others who answered the Lord's call. As we celebrate Christmas, we remember the truly courageous among us. It is a matter of courage that has brought us here today.

"Courage describes Reilly Heartwood. He came back to the town of his youth to try and make things right, even though he wasn't guilty of the many foul deeds he'd been accused of. He came home and quietly, and without reward, helped many of you through difficult times in hopes you'd forgive him. Chester Atkins said that, but for the grace of God, he'd have been consigned to the poor farm. But Chester and the rest of you will learn that it was Reilly's courage and generosity, not God, that kept you from that fate.

"Courage is something this town could use more of and that goes double for your reverend." Billy sighed and shook his head. "My brothers and sisters, I have been delivering to you the gospel for these many years without really grasping what it all meant. Knowing what the right thing is and doing it, well, they're two mighty different things."

Rose stood. "I came for an apology, not a sermon. Now you let Shep speak and we can get this over with."

"Yes, the apology," continued Billy. "Many years ago, Mary Kilgore scrubbed floors to relieve her mother of the arthritis she suffered from and years of near slavery. Mary escaped Lyle and made a new life for herself. She came back to this town and helped the sick and the dying and the homeless. She also exhibited the human flaw of vindictiveness. Today, we are asking her son, Shep, to say she was wrong, to apologize to the very person who caused his mother so much suffering."

"Stop this!" demanded Rose. "Now!"

"Shep has agreed, because he is a courageous man. He has elected to do what is right, despite all the excuses not to."

"Billy," warned Rose.

"And the reason he has to be so courageous is because your reverend is a coward. I am your pastor, but I am also an ex-con and parole violator."

The hush gave way to a wave of murmuring. It engulfed the church, drowning out Rose's cries of defeat. "This town has passed its anger and indignation to its youth like heirlooms. I'm sorry if I've let you down. But I love all of you with all my heart. I suspect I will be leaving Lyle once I have put Reilly in his grave."

Rose shuffled to the end of her pew, where she struggled to stand. I took her hand. "Wait," I said. "Please."

She glowered at me, but sat down.

I faced the congregation. "My mother was lots of things, good things. But she wasn't perfect. No one earns the right to hurt another. And so I offer to Rose my apology for the humiliation she suffered because my mother lost her compassion."

Rose climbed over the others in the pew. "This is not the apology I wrote for you." She left the church clutching her handkerchief to her mouth.

"I'm sorry that Rose is upset. And I'm sorry that many of you didn't know Reilly better. In time, I believe you will learn all that he anonymously did for you. I am here to tell you that Reilly intended to sell the poor farm before he was murdered." The last word silenced the murmuring. "I intend to do as Reilly intended."

I sat down and Billy raised his arms. "Let us pray, for Reilly and for ourselves."

It was nearly 3:00 when the last of the visitors left me alone with Frieda and Lora Jean. Hundreds in the town had passed through the house, talking about the weather and the holiday but avoiding any comment on Billy's situation, or how and why Reilly had died. Even those who had previously said horrible things about Reilly made an appearance.

At first, I thought it was hypocritical. But Billy's words about courage made me see the gesture in a different light. Even Chester said he was sorry. I told him it was time to move on. Like most of Reilly's detractors, Chester was a decent person who had reached the wrong conclusion. He would have to work hard to forgive himself for the way he had treated Reilly.

I saw Cali milling around the guests, but I only managed to catch up with her once.

"I'm sorry," I said. "I want to talk to you, but I can't seem to break free."

Cali smiled back. "Don't mind me. I'm researching my story."

A moment later, Sarah was all over me, making sure that mother's old friends were there to squeeze me—but not too hard. Everyone smiled at me and told me I had done good. I lost sight of Cali and assumed she'd left.

I had hired a half-dozen people to help with the reception

and to clean up afterwards, but Frieda wouldn't leave until everything was just right. Lora Jean gave me a hug that hurt and thanked me for helping Rodney.

"I don't like the idea of you being alone on Christmas Eve," said Frieda sincerely. "It's not right."

"I'm not alone. I have a dozen cats to keep me company. Tomorrow I'll go to the farm and have dinner with the residents."

I followed Lora Jean and Frieda to Frieda's car. "You're a good boy," she said, patting me on the cheek. "I know your mom would be busting a seam if she were here now." She was about to get inside, when she hesitated. "I don't know what's wrong with me." She handed me an envelope. "Sheriff Belamy asked me to give this to you. He said you asked for it last night."

As the car pulled from the drive, a light snow began to fall. I turned to head inside and saw Cali walking toward me, her auburn hair flecked with white flakes.

"I thought you'd left," I said.

"And where would I be going?" she said. She punctuated her question with a sigh, then kissed me.

"What was that for?"

"Research."

"I like research," I said, brushing my lips against hers. "But I have this meeting with Tom."

"I know," she said, nuzzling my ear. "This is called preliminary research."

She walked inside and I followed. While Cali fetched two glasses of wine, I sat in front of the fire and opened the envelope Frieda had given me.

"What's that?" she asked.

"Reilly's phone records. Reilly made a call to Tom Stewart's number the night he died."

"And?"

"Tom wasn't home, but the call lasted five minutes."

"Okay. Are you going to tell me what this means?"

"I'll know in a minute."

I went to the kitchen and returned with a cordless phone, then called Robbie. "When you and Amy worked on the preliminary accounting for Reilly's estate, did you or Amy go into the study where he was killed?"

"Amy wouldn't go in the room because of the blood on the couch," answered Robbie, "so I brought his records to the kitchen. Why?"

I ignored her question, asking another of my own. "Who suggested that Amy assist you?"

"She did. I thought I'd do Tom a favor and bring her along. She's actually very thorough. But you're worrying me."

"Not to worry. I'm just trying to understand something Tom said. It makes sense now. Thanks."

"So what difference does it make whether she went into the study or not?" asked Cali.

"One second," I said, then called the sheriff. I had forgotten Amy's claim that Tom had hit Reilly. Deputy Tittle answered. He wasn't excited about hearing from me. "Just one question. Did you break up a fight between Reilly and Tom Stewart?"

"Wasn't much of a fight. They were at Tom's house. Tom was giving Reilly a piece of his mind. Amy—I mean Mrs. Stewart—called me. I was nearby. When I got there, Tom pushed Reilly to the ground."

"Did Tom threaten Reilly?"

"Yeah. That's right. He threatened him."

I got the feeling again that something wasn't right. "Could I get a copy of your report?"

"I didn't file one because Reilly told me not to bother," said Tittle.

"Odd. Amy told me you filed a report."

The lie seemed to confuse Tittle. The longer he grappled with his response, the more I became certain that Amy had made up the story. "I'm not sure. I might have, but, besides, you can't see it."

I thanked the deputy and hung up.

Cali asked, "So what about Amy and the study?"

I drained my glass of wine. "Well, Reilly had a box of condoms in his study." I cleared my throat. "Amy knew where they were, meaning she must have gone through Reilly's desk when Robbie wasn't around."

I looked at my feet. I could feel Cali's eyes on me.

"You and Amy. . .?

"Kind of, yeah. She just showed up." I shook my head. "You and I weren't doing research then," I said.

Cali cut me off with a kiss. "I hope you got it out of your system."

I was considering what she meant when she asked: "Okay. So what difference does it make that she'd been in the study before?" She looked at me for a moment. "You think Amy killed Reilly?"

"I haven't been right so far," I said, but she knew that Jeb was going to tell me about Reilly wanting to sell the farm. She's the only one who knew."

"But why would she want to stop Reilly from selling the farm?"

I gave her an abbreviated version of the stories that Amy and Tom had told me. "Maybe she really didn't want Tom to displace the residents of the farm. Maybe she wanted Tom to lose the deal. I don't know, but I left Tom a message about discussing the sale of the poor farm. Amy probably listened to it. I think I better warn Tom."

Cali shook her head. "You're going to call Tom, whom you once suspected of killing Reilly, and tell him his wife, whom you slept with, is really Reilly's killer? This should be interesting."

I reached for the phone. I found Tom's business card and called the number while Cali watched me intently. To my relief, Tom answered.

"Hi, Tom. This is Shep Harrington. I was wondering if you'd have some time later today to go over in person your clients' offer to purchase the poor farm."

"Why yes," he said, obviously surprised. "But after all you've been through, I don't want you to feel pressured to act right away."

"That's very kind," I said. I thought for a moment. "Did you get the voice message I left yesterday?"

"No. Why?"

"Did you get a message from Reilly the day he died?"

The phone went silent for a long moment. "Maybe I did. I can't remember," he said, a hint of caution in his voice.

"Oh well," I said. "Not a problem. Anyway, I'd like to get this poor farm matter settled today if possible."

"Great," said Tom after a shorter pause. "I'll write up a letter of intent for you to sign when you get here."

I agreed and Tom hung up. I was about to hang up myself when I heard what I thought was breathing, then another click. I set the phone down and stared into the fire.

"So Tom is alive and you're sulking?" asked Cali.

"Something's not right," I answered.

Cali turned my head so I'd look right at her. "What's not right is that Reilly was murdered, and you don't know who killed him." I shook my head, but she persisted. "Listen to me. I admire your perceptiveness and your persistence, but this time you're not being objective. And no one expects you to be. Amy may be weird, but you don't have any proof she killed Reilly. You're reaching for closure."

Cali was right in one respect. I *was* reaching for closure. But I wasn't about to distrust my instincts. "I guess you're right," I said.

I stood up and turned to leave when Cali grabbed my elbow. "Don't think you're going without me, because you're not. I don't exactly trust you on your own."

I started to object, but Cali shook her head. I gave in, went upstairs to change my clothes, and met Cali outside. A light dusting of snow coated the driveway and the flakes were getting bigger.

Tom and Amy Stewart lived a few miles outside of town in a colonial that tried too hard to look antebellum. I pressed the doorbell and waited. A moment later, Tom appeared and invited us both in. I introduced Cali but ignored the question on Tom's face about who she might be. As we stepped into the foyer, Cali gave me a knowing glance, as if to point out that Tom was still alive and kicking.

Tom led us through the foyer and into a large, dimly-lit room that I guessed was his office. Along the left wall was a large rosewood desk flanked by two floor-to-ceiling windows. A halogen lamp illuminated the desk, but very little else. Along the center of the right wall was a fireplace with a stone mantle and hearth. A fire crackled and hissed. The flames filled the room with dancing shadows. I could feel its heat even a dozen feet away.

Tom moved two chairs in front of the desk. "Shall we get started?"

Before Cali and I could take our seats, Amy appeared. "By all means, let's get started," she interjected. "Perhaps you can evict the residents of the poor farm before Christmas."

"Amy, please," said Tom. "Nothing like that is going to happen."

She walked stiffly into the room, her hands pressed into the pockets of a heavy knit sweater. She stopped and stared into the fire, the flames giving her face a strange orange hue.

Tom went to her. He put his arm around her, but she pulled back. "Reilly said the same thing," she said, her voice wavering, her eyes still fixed on the fire. "He pleaded with me, but he was lying. Men are such liars."

"Shut up, Amy," commanded Tom.

I felt Cali's hands on my shoulders, then felt her press against me. I reached back and pulled her hands down to my waist. "What's happening?" she whispered.

"I think she's gone over the edge," I said. "We'd better get out of here."

"Reilly left a message for Tom," said Amy. "I erased it, then went to the house with Tom's gun."

"Stop, Amy," pleaded Tom. "You don't know what you're saying. No one can prove you did anything."

Amy ignored him. "I let myself in, then heard a gun shot. I saw a boy run out. I hoped he'd done the job for me, but he hadn't. Reilly was sitting on the couch, struggling with his crutches. It was just a matter of picking up the kid's gun and pulling the trigger. I protected those old people. I saved them and myself. It was a noble act. But you . . ."

She turned and looked into Tom's eyes. I knew at that moment what was about to happen, but before I could move, the room was filled with a flash and the angry blast of a handgun. Tom staggered backwards, his face locked in a grimace of shock that would be his death mask. Amy turned toward Cali and me as smoke wafted from a small hole in her sweater.

I started to move, but Amy raised her gun. "I tried to tell you that the poor farm couldn't be sold. You didn't listen. If you'd only listened."

I pulled Cali's hands from my chest and pushed them to the small of my back. A moment later, Cali found the grip on the gun wedged behind my waistband. I shifted my weight as she pulled the gun free. "But I did listen," I said. "I made arrangements for the residents to live in Reilly's house."

She stared at me from behind dead eyes. "I should have hit you harder."

I felt Cali's hand on my buttocks, then felt the barrel of the gun slide between my legs. I hoped Cali and I would someday have time to reflect on the Freudian implications of this exchange. I rubbed my hands on my legs, then brought my left hand to my cheek. Amy watched me like a hawk. I was about to reach for the gun with my right hand, but the grip of the gun swung downward and the weapon slid to my knees. I knew that I couldn't hold it for long.

"It's time," said Amy, "to end this."

"We should pray," I said to Cali.

I felt Cali hesitate, guessing, I suppose, that her best chance for escape was standing, not kneeling. But as I lowered myself to the floor, I could feel her going with me.

What followed took only a moment, but seemed to occur in slow motion. I grabbed my gun with my right hand at the same time as I took hold of Cali's coat in my left. I pulled her forward and dove to my right. The gunshot sounded like cannon fire. I felt a burning sensation on my left side and the air leaving my lungs.

As I touched the floor, another explosion echoed through the room and a flash of light burst from my right hand. In the light from the fireplace, I saw Amy drop her weapon and clutch her abdomen. But she could not slow a circle of darkness that spread across her white sweater with amazing speed. As Amy crumpled to the floor, I heard Cali scream. Then darkness engulfed me for what I thought would be the last time.

Epilogue

Reilly's was not the last funeral Lyle would endure that holiday season. On New Year's Eve, Amy and Tom were lowered into the snow-covered ground a hundred feet from Reilly's grave. The Reverend Billy performed the service. A small group of attorneys from D.C. braved the wind and blowing snow to attend the graveside service, or so I was told. I didn't go. I took no pleasure in the deaths of Tom and Amy Stewart. But I didn't go so far as to forgive them.

Sheriff Belamy had to arrest the Reverend Billy for violating parole. The town was in an uproar, until Providence stepped in to save the day. The prison where Billy had been incarcerated had burned down and his records lost. As far as the law was concerned, he had paid for his crime and was a free man.

I spent the holidays in the hospital recuperating from a collapsed lung and broken ribs, the result of the bullet that nearly ended my life. Cali kept me from going crazy in the hospital by reading to me and watching movies with me. We did not speak about the fact that I had killed Amy. I wrestled with that issue privately, and still do from time to time.

Around the end of January, Cali published two stories, one about Reilly and one about me. The articles were picked up nationally, and she received job offers from big, prestigious newspapers and magazines around the country.

Despite Cali's natural investigative instincts, the full truth about Reilly and Mary will probably never be known. The only historical evidence of the events that led up to their separation is a letter written by Reilly to the Reverend James Tyler, Mattie Devereaux's brother. Mattie said that the letter explained what caused them to separate. While the letter made some facts clear, it left the mystery of what happened intact.

In her article, Cali noted that because Reilly and Mary were buried side-by-side, they were closer in death than they had been in life. Death, it seemed, had not parted them, but joined them for all eternity. Cali also wrote that the truth about the two lovers appears in the words to "Lonesome Song." Following her article, the song hit the top of the charts again.

Cali and I had become good friends, meaning we were involved but not committed. We both knew that her career was her highest priority. She had earned a second chance to pursue her dream, and I had no desire to stand in her way. She left late in the spring to find another story worth telling. As of this moment, I haven't heard that she found one.

Around March, the developer announced that the financing for the shopping mall had fallen through and with it the deal for the poor farm. But the residents, along with Terry and his wife, had already moved to Reilly's house. I like my privacy, so I moved to the poor farm. *Bottom line:* the residents live in a mansion in town with all the amenities, while I, a millionaire, live on a farm that sports a dungeon rumored to be inhabited by ghosts. The farmhouse is actually quite comfortable the way it is, but I will admit that Cali and I have spent more than one rainy day drawing up plans for a solarium, a spa, a tennis court, and an indoor pool.

Despite Cali's best efforts and the support of many others, I fell into a deep depression just after New Year. The common opinion was that I was suffering delayed shock from all that had happened. But what I couldn't admit to anyone was how angry I was with everyone—the townsfolk, Reilly, my mother, the Stewarts, the people who put me in jail. I was pissed, and because the anger wasn't focused, I had no way to deal with it.

It was a gift of a bunch of bananas from Doc that opened my eyes. The fruit arrived with a card that said only, "I'm sorry."

For lots of "reasons," I had avoided Doc up to that point. In doing so, I condemned him to carry the burden of his mistake in perpetuity. By not forgiving him, I had also condemned myself to smolder with anger forever. Life, I eventually realized, wasn't long enough for such foolishness. When I dropped in on Doc and embraced him, I imagined two monkeys fleeing into the jungle.

A few weeks later, Billy used the monkey-banana theme in a sermon and invited each member of the congregation to forgive someone. Billy then handed Terry a banana and confessed he'd prayed that Terry would hurt his bowling hand. Since then, bananas have become the preferred fruit of contrition in Lyle.

I applied for reinstatement to the Virginia Bar and was notified on Valentine's Day that my request had been granted. I greeted the news with ambivalence.

Since high school, I had wanted to be a lawyer. I became enamored with the profession's trappings of success—an expensive house, country club membership, powerful car, and designer suits. Being disbarred had been almost as painful to me as being locked up. I went through the reinstatement process because I wanted to be vindicated, and because I thought it was my way back to my old life.

Now that I'm licensed to practice law again, I'm not so sure I want my old life back. I don't covet things, and I have no desire to be with people I once considered friends but who abandoned me when my trial began.

When I finally accepted the fact that I was going to prison, I was frightened on many levels. Prison was going to change my life in many obvious ways. I realize, now, that the fortune Reilly left me also has the power to change me, but in ways far more subtle than going to prison. I am grateful, of course, but wary. I don't want money to make me into someone I've always despised.

One of the obvious attributes of wealth is what it creates. Thanks to Reilly, I have choices—maybe too many choices. I once thought if I were filthy rich, I'd feel liberated. Maybe that would be true if I'd earned my money. But Reilly's bequest to me sometimes feels like a burden. He supported more causes than I can name, and each has called asking for assurances that I will continue "Reilly's good work." And the list of charities wanting to be on the Reilly plan grows daily. Having the power to do good is an awesome responsibility, and I've only begun to understand why Reilly decided to do it quietly.

At this moment, I'm living in Lyle wearing blue jeans and sweatshirts and driving an old Honda. No blue suits. No tennis courts. No one to suck up to. Instead, I'm surrounded by the people of Lyle—people who are intimately involved with each other, who imperfectly interact and affect each other. But for all their flaws, the residents of Lyle are indeed alive.

And for the first time in years, so am I.

Chain Thinking

1

Except for the unusually cool weather, August first was like most of my mornings. By seven, I had showered, dressed, and finished breakfast, and was sitting on the porch nursing a second cup of coffee, when I noticed a cloud of dust rising above the trees that lined the long driveway to my house. Moments later, a car sped out of the plume, its rear end fishtailing in the soft dirt. If I had known who was in the car and why, if I could have foreseen how allowing this visitor into my home was going to affect my life, I might have gone inside and refused to answer the door. And Thinking back, I should have realized that only bad news travels this early and this fast.

As the car slid to a halt at the edge of the lawn, I bolted from my chair, stopping at the edge of the porch. stood. For a long moment, no one emerged, leaving me to muse that maybe the car was driverless. But then a door swung open with a loud screech and the driver, dressed in a burgundy cloak with an oversized hood, appeared. I had no doubt that my visitor was female. The soft fabric moved as she walked, clinging to her subtle curves, so much so that I wasn't sure if the cloak was all she was wearing. Her face was hidden behind a dark oval shadow, but I stared into the darkness anyway.

Chain Thinking *Excerpt*

When she reached the porch, she asked, "You are a lawyer?" She spoke with an affectation that was sensual, almost arousing.

"Yes," I replied. "My name is Shep Harrington. Who are you looking for?"

A moment passed. I heard her sigh inside her cocoon. I watched, enthralled. Then she said, "An attorney who went to prison."

Ouch! I had never considered my stay in prison a prerequisite to employment.

"That would be me," I said. "Unless, of course, you're carrying a sickle."

I heard a quick laugh, but she didn't move. A moment passed and she pushed back her hood.

I don't think I flinched, but I'm not absolutely certain. Seen from her right profile, she could be mistaken for a model, perhaps in the middle of her career, but still physically attractive by any objective measures. But the left side of her face had been burned, damaging her eye and ear, and causing the corner of her mouth to turn downward. Despite the damage, something about her seemed familiar, if only remotely so.

She waited quietly for a moment. I sensed this was to allow me time to assimilate the damage to her face and to consider what it might be like to be in her situation. Finally, she asked, "You were expecting Snow White?"

The question had a practiced quality, originating not from some well-wallowed pool of self-pity, but from an inner strength. She was challenging me, trying to disarm me, using her misfortune to gain advantage. I admired her immediately, and raised the ante.

"I wasn't," I replied evenly, "but neither was I expecting the Phantom of the Opera." She glared at me, and I at her. Finally, her face brightened, and she laughed softly. "What can I do for you, Miss...?"

"What makes you think I'm not married?" Her eyes drilled into mine, then she laughed with such amusement that I couldn't help but laugh too. The mirth, however, was short-lived.

"My name is Sydney Vail. I don't have much time. I don't have any time." Her voice quaked as she spoke. "I need your help."

"Are you in trouble?"

She shook her head. "I don't need your legal advice." She glanced at the car. "I work with animals that need help. Reilly Heartwood used to assist me sometimes. With Reilly dead, I didn't know where to go."

"So you need money?"

"I have an animal that needs a safe place to stay for a few days."

"I don't know much about caring for sick animals," I said. "Surely you know other people who are far more qualified."

Sydney stared at me. "Kikora is not sick," she replied, her voice strident and demanding. "She is in danger. There is no one else. I have no choice. You have to help me. Come with me."

"Wait a minute," I snapped. "Slow down."

"I don't have time for an interrogation," said Sydney, looking at me impatiently. "Call Frieda," she said. "She'll vouch for me. But please hurry."

Frieda Hahn had been Reilly Heartwood's housekeeper before his death last Christmas. I was both the executor of his estate and his primary beneficiary. I went inside and called the house. Given the early hour, Frieda assumed that something bad had happened. "Nothing's wrong," I said. "I have a lady here named Sydney Vail. She's asking for my help, and she says you'll confirm that Reilly had helped her on other occasions."

Frieda was suddenly quiet. "She has a scar on her face?"

The question seemed understated, given the extent of Sydney's injuries. "Yes."

"It's okay. Give her what she needs."

I hung up the phone. "Okay," I said to Sydney. "I'm game."

I followed her to the car and she opened the back door. When she turned around, I thought she was holding a baby. Only after a moment did I realize Kikora was a young chimpanzee.

"She's asleep because I had to drug her to calm her down," said Sydney. "I have written instructions on what you need to do, how to feed her, and what to expect. I have some supplies in the trunk."

"I'm sorry," I said. "I can't do this. I don't know anything about chimps, you, or...."

"Do you want her to die?" Sydney looked at me, tears in her eyes. "You are my only hope. You've got to trust me."

Kikora stirred and stared at me sleepily through large brown eyes. I was transfixed by the sadness and fear that I saw there. Sydney touched Kikora's cheek, then looked at me. "I will call you in a few days. I promise. This will all make sense." She kissed me on the cheek, then got back in her car.

Kikora and I watched from the edge of the lawn as Sydney sped down the road until a cloud of dust obscured her car. I heard Kikora whimper, then felt her tighten her grip around my neck. Fifteen minutes earlier, I had been drinking coffee, still waiting for the day to unfold in the way that I had planned.

Life assumes a certain rhythm. The sun rises and sets, and in between we go about our affairs according to our own whims and desires, oblivious to complex equations of cause and effect, finding comfort in the illusion that we are in control of our destiny. Sometimes, we arrive at a fork in the road and must choose one over another without knowing where either leads. Sometimes, the fork is chosen for us.

In just a few minutes that Monday morning, almost involuntarily, I had become a foster parent to a chimpanzee. Sydney said she would be back and all would make sense. Holding Kikora, I could only wonder.

2

Kikora was awake but still groggy from the sedative Sydney had given her. I put her on the couch and sat next to her. Looking at her sweet face, it was difficult to see why a sedative was required. I stroked her back and she regarded me curiously through heavy eyes. "So," I said. "Here we are."

All I knew about chimpanzees I'd learned from watching television, and nothing I'd seen described how to care for a real chimp. I opened the bag Sydney had left and inventoried its contents. What Sydney had described as instructions were three typed pages of do's and don'ts with notes scrawled in the margins. I found a copy of Family Tree, a book by Jane Roth, a half-dozen diapers, a bag of apples, several boxes of popcorn, an assortment of brushes, and lots of ribbons. I glanced at the back cover of the Roth book and then at Kikora. "We're cousins," I said, rubbing her back. She looked at me through large sad eyes, her breathing labored.

I found located a towel and slipped it under Kikora, then went into the kitchen to clean the dishes. Twenty minutes later, a hooting Kikora was jumping on the couch. When I approached, she screeched and darted away.

After an hour of chasing, pleading, and baiting, I managed

Chain Thinking *Excerpt*

to trap Kikora in a windowless pantry. I called Frieda and told her I needed her to come out to the farm. I did my best to deflect her questions, then raised more by asking that Cecil and Harry Drake join her, and that they bring their tools.

A half hour later, I heard Frieda call for me. I answered from the dining room, and Frieda, Cecil, and Harry appeared. Carrie Toliver appeared showed up an instant later. They stood in a line, gawking at the mess that lay before them. Curtains were lying in heaps on the floor. The curtain rods had been pulled from the walls, leaving gaping holes in the plaster. A chandelier was dangling precariously over the dining room table by a single wire. The chairs were on their backs, partially covered by the table-cloth.

Cecil and Harry Drake are twins. I suspect they are in their sixties, but even they aren't sure when they were born. Other than their ages and a knack for working with their hands, they have little in common. Harry is tall, energetic, and engaging. Cecil is heavyset and aloof to the point of seeming dimwitted. I say "seeming" because Cecil is, in actuality, an expert carpenter and mechanic. I suspect his lights are on but the curtain is drawn.

Carrie Toliver Tolliver is a small, almost frail woman with a sweet face and a head of cotton-white hair. She believes she's eighty-two, but she, too, isn't absolutely sure. Whatever her age, Carrie is deceptively perceptive, disarmingly witty, and strong willed.

The reason for the uncertainty in their ages is that until last Christmas, they were the forgotten residents of the last poor farm operating in Virginia, the same farm I now call home. Cecil and Harry first came to the farm as children after their parents died in a fire. Carrie is the only resident to have been born on the farm. A fourth resident, Jamie Wren, is a quiet, reclusive man who composes offbeat sayings for fortune cookies and greeting cards that appeal to city folk. No one knows when he first came to the farm or why.

The path leading me to the farm and sending the Residents residents to live in Lyle is complicated, but the short version is that

Reilly Heartwood, a country singer performing and recording under the stage name "C.C. Hollinger," bequeathed to me the farm, a mansion in town (named "Heartwood House" for obvious reasons), and an estate worth tens of millions of dollars. Before his funeral, I agreed to sell the farm to a developer and move the residents to the mansion in town. I intended to go back to live in my home outside Washington, D.C., but instead ended up in a local hospital with a gunshot wound to my chest. By the time I recovered, I had no reason to leave Lyle and many reasons to stay. By chance, the deal for the poor farm fell through. Because I like my privacy, I moved to the poor farm. Bottom line: the four residents of the poor farm — Cecil, Harry, Carrie, and Jamie — live with Fried Hahn, Reilly's former housekeeper, and Lora Jean Brady, a previously homeless teenager, at Reilly's amenity-laden mansion, while I live on a farm sporting a dungeon rumored to be inhabited by ghosts. Still, the farm is my home and the people who reside at Heartwood House are my family. Kikora could have done far worse than to end up here.

"What happened?" asked Cecil.

A crashing sound came from the kitchen. "Outside everyone, and I will explain."

"Have you been drinking?" asked Frieda.

"Not yet," I said, "but hold the thought."

I managed to get everyone onto the porch and seated. "I need your help," I said.

"Will you please tell me what's happened here?" demanded Frieda.

"I'm getting to that," I replied, "but first I need you to understand that if you get involved, you may be committing a crime, at least technically. Even if you say no, you'll be a potential witness to a crime I may be committing. That means that I need you to be very careful not to talk to anyone about what I'm going to ask you."

"What kind of crime?" asked Cecil.

"Possession of stolen property," I said. "Perhaps some kind of accessory charge."

"I don't know," said Harry. "I've never committed a crime before."

"It sounds exciting," said Carrie.

"Stop with this chatter and get to the point," commanded Frieda.

"I need your help taking care of a baby chimp," I said simply.

Frieda stared at me knowingly. I believe she knew the answer, but she asked the next question anyway. "And where did you get this chimp?"

I shrugged. "From Sydney Vail," I responded.

Frieda was relentless. "And what in God's wisdom possessed you to agree to something so stupid?"

The eyes of Carrie, Cecil, and Harry focused on me, anticipating an answer. Another loud crash came from inside the house, but no one moved. "Because you told me to do what she asked?" I said, my answer sounding like a question.

Frieda glared at me. "I thought she was asking you for money. Reilly used to give her money. He'd never agree to take care of a monkey."

"Kikora is a chimpanzee," I said.

No one spoke for a moment. Frieda looked at the floor, her shoulders drooping. "All right," she said. "You have a chimpanzee. Why would that be a crime?"

"Because it's likely that Sydney stole the chimp," I replied. "Possession of stolen property is against the law. If we knowingly assist Sydney in getting away with theft, or even burglary, we could be considered accessories after the fact."

"If Sydney was involved, then I guess she stole it," said Frieda nodding. "And I guess Sydney told you that the chimp's life was in danger?"

"Yup."

"Every animal that Sydney helps is in danger of losing its life," said Frieda. "I don't know how Reilly could deal with a woman who goes around stealing animals for a living."

"My only other choice is to call the cops," I said, "and set the criminal justice system in motion. I've had my taste of that system, and I'm not inclined to sic it on anyone unless I'm certain they deserve it. I'm willing to take the risk of breaking the law for a few days until Sydney returns, but each one of you has to decide on your own."

"I think we should help Shep with his chimp," said Carrie. "Reilly would have wanted it that way."

"I'd like to help," said Harry.

Frieda shook her head. "As if I don't have enough work caring for the homeless as it is. So what do you need?"

"Wait here," I said.

I went inside and opened the pantry door. Kikora was sitting in a pile of paper and cans. She had found a box of graham crackers and was busily trying to break through the plastic wrap that covered the package. I took a key from my pocket, slit the plastic, and offered her a cracker. Then I took her hand and walked her outside to meet the others.

"This is Kikora," I said.

"Oh my," said Carrie. "Look at her. She's just a baby."

"Who likes to swing and climb," I said. I gave Kikora another cracker, then handed the instruction book to Frieda. "Make a list of what we need from the instructions. I'll pay for it." I explained to Cecil and Harry that they needed to make the bunkhouse as chimp-proof as possible.

"Who's going to watch her at night?" asked Carrie. "She might not like being alone."

"I think she'll do fine in the bunkhouse," I said. I saw the empathy in Carrie's eyes. "You can stay here if you'd like."

"We'll take turns," said Harry.

"We can install video cameras in the bunkhouse," said Cecil. "I saw a set of wireless cameras advertised on the Web for a few hundred bucks."

"That's a lot of money," said Harry.

"It's not a lot of money," responded Cecil. His face lit up with a devilish smile. "Besides, it isn't my money. It's Shep's."

For the next hour, I straightened up the dining room while

Cecil and Harry figured out what they needed to convert the bunkhouse into a chimp-proof room. Frieda made her list while complaining about how she always had to clean up after other people's mistakes. Carrie brushed Kikora and talked to her. All seemed under control until Kikora decided that it was playtime again. For her next romp, she bolted outside and up a hundred-foot oak as if it had stairs. When she was a few feet from the top, she perched on a branch and hooted.

"Now what do we do?" asked Carrie.

"Make popcorn," I said, "and hope she gets tired."

Praise for Lonesome Song

"As a retired high school science teacher, and a self-confessed mysteryholic, I thoroughly enjoyed *Lonesome Song*. Its opener is a great hook. Its end is smashingly good. And, in between, there are characters to care about, plot developments that surprise, a mystery that well sustains itself, and sly humor that works. Take it from me: A visit to *Lonesome Song* is well worth your time."—*Ginnie Levin, Baltimore, MD*

"Shep Harrington is an engagingly human hero and *Lonesome Song* is a rich read."—*Bob Cullen, author of A Mulligan for Bobby Jobe*

"I found myself enjoying *Lonesome Song* immensely. I loved the main character's main challenge—getting a proper burial for his good friend. I loved the confrontation between the old lady Rose and the main character Shep—and the whole old-grudge factor. The scene where the two lab-characters come in and push rods through the corpse was riveting. Everything ended in satisfactory manner. And the main character is one I'd like to know better. His characteristics of sleeplessness—of a hardening brought on by incarceration, and at the time of *Lonesome Song*, his manly need to be with a woman—all make for someone I'd want to see again in a sequel. Yet, *Lonesome Song* is more than the sum of its wonderful parts. Purely and simply, it makes for a rollicking and unpredictable read."—*Jeff Boison, Editor-in-chief, www.pindeldyboz.com*

"As someone who's read thousands upon thousands of mysteries during a 75-year lifetime, at a pace of about one every two days, I enthusiastical ly recommend Elliott Light's unusual but entertaining *Lonesome Song*. A couple of things made it quite different from many of those I've read, yet every bit as good as the best of them. First, it took me half the time to read as the usual mystery. Second, its premise was unique—a famous man dies but can't be buried. Third, its small town setting was rare, pleasant, and central to the story. Like the best of the best mysteries, it not only maintained the mystery throughout, but I cared about *Lonesome Song's* characters—from the deceased Reilly Heartwood, to the protagonist Shep Harrington. And, like the best of the mysteries I've read, Lonesome Song was also about themes that are both universal and important—from the power of forgiveness to the weaknesses of the criminal justice system. I don't often recommend the mysteries I read, but I make an exception for *Lonesome Song*. Read it and you'll give yourself a very special and enjoyable afternoon."—*Rita Bortz, Hallandale, Florida*

"My sister let me read an advance copy of your book. I hope you don't mind. *Lonesome Song* was excellent. I thoroughly enjoyed the road you took me down. Thanks for a great six hours."—*Alexander (Alex) Siahpoosh, psychologist*

"If I had to use one word to describe *Lonesome Song*, it would have to be fantastic! And I don't even like fiction! From the first few paragraphs, you know something fishy is going on. In the beginning, each chapter drives the mystery deeper. In the middle, all bets are off as to who actually committed the crime and why. And towards the end, each chapter reveals additional clues as to who murdered Reilly. I really liked the cast of characters that Elliott Light has assembled. There is someone for everyone to identify with. Needless to say, I am greatly looking forward to the next Shep Harrington mystery."—*Eric Gibson, Leesburg, Virginia*

"Elliott Light's first suspenseful novel is rich in content and even richer in character development. Cali McBride, a reporter and love interest for Shep Harrington, the Light-created lawyer/sleuth, best describes the book's essence: 'A story about a famous recording artist, a town that won't bury him, and the hint of foul play has *Rolling Stone* written all over it. Then throw in an attorney who once was the poster boy for government fraud, and this story will rock.' *Lonesome Song* is an easy but enriching read. I look forward to reading more from the author and from Shep."—*Martin E. Silfen, entertainment attorney (Mays & Valentine, Va. Beach), law professor (William & Mary), and author (Law and Business of the Entertainment Industries)*

"For me, *Lonesome Song* was a good, casual, interesting read that kept my attention from beginning to end. I was curious throughout as to 'whodunnit,' and I found myself speculating until the conclusion on the possible motives of the array of characters. The end, which I won't spoil, was heart-warming."— *Rosemary Maione*

"What a delightful book, populated with unique characters, a compelling mystery, and an intriguing plot that kept me in suspense right to the end! Having lived in Northern Virginia (Burke when it was still farmland) and hiked all over hell and gone in Virginia and West Virginia, I could see the settings in my head and only imagine that perhaps I'd driven past a poor farm where your drama played out unseen by me and all the others speeding by, somewhere on I-66. Thanks for giving me the opportunity to read this. I look forward to reading a lot more of these in the years to come."—*Lewis Perdue, author of the acclaimed mystery-thriller "Daughter of God" and the guidebook "Country Inns of Maryland, Virginia & West Virginia"*

"*Lonesome Song*, with its cast of odd characters and its collection of strange situations, was great! Its small town setting of Lyle typifies every small Virginia town I know. And there's a new twist lurking around every corner. I guess you won't be surprised when I say I'm looking forward to more Shep!"— *Chris Lynn, Front Royal, VA*

"As soon as you turn the first few pages of *Lonesome Song*, you can't help but feel for Shep and become involved in his character. His hardened sarcastic wisdom and accurate observations resonate with any of us who are exposed to the law. The good people of Lyle need a good shaking, and Shep Harrington does it! He can practice in my firm any time."—*Jon L. Roberts, Roberts Abokhair & Mardula, LLC, Reston, VA*

"*Lonesome Song* is a real page-turner. Once I started, I couldn't put it down and finished it in an afternoon. It will be a great beach book, or a great read for an airplane, train, or bus ride. I'm looking forward to seeing what mischief you have in store for Shep—and Cali—in the next edition."—*Deb Joseph, Herndon, VA; Manager, Customer Relationship Management (CRM) Systems; and "avid bibliophile"*

"As someone who reads mystery stories to keep from getting bored, I found Elliott Light's book a refreshing change. Its fast-paced story offers more food for thought and literacy than the average sample of this genre. Light offers philosophical musings that lend depth to the story, and the characters, any one of which can be found in your own neighborhood, speak to the reader, as does the small-town setting. At the same time, this is a mystery story that moves right along, and captures the reader's attention. Light, in this his first book, has shown us that he has considerable insight into and a solid grasp of the wiles of human nature. I strongly recommend '*Lonesome Song*' and am hoping for a sequel."—*Ed Dager, Professor Emeritus (Sociology), University of Maryland*

"I just finished reading your book and thoroughly enjoyed it. I'm an avid fan of hard-boiled detective novels, and your book has a great style and easy manner that makes me miss the Shenendoahs. You did a great job of creating your characters, and keeping the outcome a mystery. There were enough people who wanted to get rid of Reilly, but you supplied a nice twist that I didn't see coming."—*David Jaynes, Airport General Manager, WHSmith Travel USA, Waterstone Booksellers, Los Angeles, CA*

"I recently finished reading *Lonesome Song*, which I had a hard time putting down. I've read several series of famous mystery writers, and they all seem to be done in the same monotone, using standard interviews with predictable suspects, and always suggesting that lots of people could have done the deed. *Lonesome Song*, while a mystery, was very fresh and twisty. I found myself continuously grinning at its clever writing. I liked how I was launched into the drama right away. I loved the description of the characters, especially those of Amy and Rose. And Shep seemed truly honest and human. I smiled ear to ear when he took the body and got an autopsy going! I can't wait to get my hands on the sequel." —*KC Caselli, California*

"A good, old-fashioned, thoroughly captivating whodunnit, complete with wrongs of the past made right, dark humor, sins of the father, etc. I can't wait until the next episode in Shep's saga!"—*Paladin J. Henderson, Special Agent, US Air Force*

Acknowledgements

I wish to express my gratitude to the following people who took the time to read *Lonesome Song* and to offer comments, suggestions, and encouragement: Alex Buckley, Ginnie Levin, Bob Cullen, Jeff Boison, Rita Bortz, Alex Siahpoosh, Alexa Raad, Eric Gibson, Martin E. Silfen, Rosemary Maione, Lewis Perdue, Chris Lynn, Deb Joseph, Ed Dager, David Jaynes, Katy Caselli, and Paladin Henderson.

I offer a special thank you to Arlen "Ray" Wilson, who not only read various drafts of *Lonesome Song* but drafts of early novels and managed to find something constructive to say about all of them, and to Theresa Williams for her dedicated effort on the galley and text layout. The stunning cover is the work of Steven Parke (design) and John Phillips (photography).

Small publishers offer the unpublished writer a chance to step into the light. Bruce Bortz, the publisher of *Lonesome Song*, loves bringing books to life. Without him, *Lonesome Song* would be another mass of bits encoded on a hard drive. I'm not sure how you thank someone for making a dream come true.

Surrounded by friends and supporters, a want-to-be writer still needs someone who will tell the truth about a sentence, a chapter, or a book. Sonya, my ever patient but none too shy partner, is that person. For most of our twenty years together, she has endured the raw first cut of the latest new idea, the discouragement that comes from rejection, and the isolation that writing demands. We are sharing this fantasy together because she sets the bar high, then moves it up a notch. (Reminds me a bit of Cali—hmmmmm).